NOBODY DROWNS IN MINERAL LAKE

A Novel by

Michael B. Druxman

1958

The body had been in the water since midnight, riding the waves as they repeatedly slammed it against huge black boulders. Lake water had invaded its now bloodless gashes. By the time the sun's first rays caught the remains, the cadaver looked as white as the upturned belly of a very dead fish.

A crop duster flew over shortly before eight, then circled back at a lower altitude to get a closer look. Sure of what he'd seen, the pilot increased his speed and turned his plane eastward.

It was twenty minutes later when the beach residents heard the siren heading in their direction.

Sam Jackson was laying out page three when the siren screamed past his office. He didn't have time to go chasing after fire engines this morning, but this week's edition of the *Mineral Lake Bulletin* still needed news copy. The dusty-haired editor wiped his hands on a scrap of newsprint, tossed it down among the half-dozen others on the floor, then he took up his cold stogie from an ashtray, and headed for the door after the emergency vehicle.

Jackson was dressed in his regular business attire: gray wrinkled slacks, loose-fitting white shirt, his protruding gut overflowing his belt, and the unchangeable eyeshade.

He hadn't shaved. He seldom did on Sundays, since nobody in the town paid much attention to his neighbor's appearance anyway. His two-day beard made him look older than his fifty-one years.

It was odd, he thought, that he hadn't heard the air raid signal. Mineral Lake's population of just under twenty-five hundred was barely able to maintain its second-hand fire engine. It had an all-volunteer fire department, and whenever one of the frequent reports of a brush blaze was called into the town's one-story combination city hall/sheriff's department/ fire station, the deafening civil-defense warning informed a half-dozen male residents that their services were needed.

On the other hand, perhaps it *hadn't* been the fire truck.

Jackson had locked the door from the inside. He always did when he came into work on Sundays. It took him a few seconds to find the right key among the dozen or so on the heavy ring he carried in his pocket.

Main Street, with its muddle of drab storefronts and ill-kept hotels, was devoid of activity on this crisp morning. It was only 8:20, according to the editor's watch, and, unless they were going to church, few people would be out. It was, after all, mid-October and the tourists were long gone.

Across the way from the modest brown brick building that housed his operation, 78-year-old Lila Seltzer, one of the many permanent residents of the Crocker Rest Home, had wandered out onto the sidewalk to see what was happening. Sam had known the widow for nearly five years, and he did not want to be drawn into one of her long-winded conversations.

"Which way did it go?" he called.

The shriveled woman in the pink housecoat didn't say a word, but pointed up the hill toward the west end of town.

"Fire engine?"

Again, she remained silent, just shrugged her shoulders. Sam thought she must have laryngitis.

He spotted the 11-year-old Watkins boy at the top of
the mild incline, standing out in front of the Presbyterian
church. "Hey, Donny," he yelled. "What's going on?"

The freckled-faced youth, who had been gazing off to
the west, ran down the hill. "It was the sheriff," he shouted.
"He went by here in one hell of a hurry!"

It was probably nothing at all. Elmer Olsen was
slapping his wife around again; somebody was trespassing on
Harry Barnett's west beach; or it was some other piece of
news Sam couldn't write about, lest he offend too many of his
subscribers. Yet, he, at least, had to tag along after the
authorities to see if there was by chance a usable story.

He checked his watch again as he climbed into his
new 1958 Ford coupe. Arlene, his wife, would be in church
for another half-hour and, unless the sheriff found something
important, he would be back in plenty of time to drive her
home from services. She was planning an early supper this
afternoon, then he'd promised to take her to the local movie
house to see *The Young Lions*. He really didn't like films
much, but she'd read the book, felt motherly toward
Montgomery Clift, and had her heart set on seeing the picture.

Making a U-turn in the middle of the block, Jackson
headed west. The sheriff's car was nowhere in sight as he
topped the hill overlooking the town's haphazardly planned
residential section with its scattering of middle class cottages.
He drove slowly, checking every side street in an effort to
catch a glimpse of it.

He knew this was probably a wild goose chase, but
Sam relished the pursuit. The experience brought back
memories of his days with the *San Francisco Chronicle*, when
the first-string newsmen had been inducted or re-assigned as
war correspondents. He'd been pulled off the rewrite desk to
cover the police beat. Both he and his editor knew his writing
style lacked the flair for front page reporting. The assignment

would only be temporary, but the eighteen months he'd spent siren chasing was the most exciting period of his life.

At First Street, Jackson's car almost smashed into burly Charley Nathan, city councilman, and one of Mineral Lake's four realtors. The balding civic leader was rushing across Main, his shirt open, paying no attention to traffic.

"Jesus Christ!" Sam slammed on the brakes.

The sixty-year-old Nathan remained indifferent to the screeching that would have made most men leap to safety. He maintained his lumbering sprint down First, then cut across Harry Barnett's twenty-acre vacant lot, heading toward the west beach.

"Charley!" the editor shouted out the window at his best advertising customer. "You trying to get killed!?!"

Jackson saw where Nathan was going. A block away, parked next to the chain link fence that kept sunbathers off Barnett's private beach, was the sheriff's car, its red light flashing.

He backed up the Ford, made a sharp right onto First, and arrived at the eight-foot high fence just ahead of the councilman.

"We got trouble," puffed Charley as Sam emerged from his vehicle.

"What's up?

Nathan's reply was interrupted by Ed LaGrange, tall, strapping deputy sheriff, who had been staring through a pair of binoculars toward the middle of the lake. "I think there's a dead body out there," he announced, not quite sure how to handle the situation. "It's about two or three hundred yards off shore, by the bluff."

"I know," said Charley. "The operator called me."

"How can I get onto the beach?" LaGrange brushed his generous crop of blonde hair off his forehead. "Did Mr. Barnett leave a gate key with somebody in case of emergencies?"

"Climb over!" ordered Charley.

"There's barbed wire on top. Maybe I could shoot the lock off."

"Shit!' said Nathan. He wished to hell he wasn't the ranking city official on the scene. "Go ahead. Do that. I'll call Harry personally and explain what happened."

Sam knew the thirty-one-year-old officer was still uncertain, and he understood why. Ed wasn't really a cop. He was the local jeweler who worked Sundays as relief for Sheriff Oscar Heath. His only qualifications for the position were his size and the fact that he'd been a member of the Navy Shore Patrol. He was paid ten dollars for cruising the town's usually quiet streets, and occasionally issuing a stern warning to mischievous kids. When he'd accepted the job seven months ago to help make ends meet, he probably never figured he'd have to deal with a drowning.

"You'd better get somebody from the hospital down here, Ed," suggested the former police reporter. "They're going to have to do a medical report, you know."

LaGrange singled out a lanky youth with an acne-marked face from the crowd of two dozen gawking citizens. "Gene, run up the block," he said, gesturing toward the closest house. "Call Mason Hospital. Ask them to send down a doctor and an ambulance."

He turned to the councilman. "Did anybody try to reach the sheriff?"

"Operator said he wasn't home. Said he was fishing over at Blue Lake."

Jackson could see that with the only real lawman absent and these two well-meaning officials out of their element, he was going to have to take hold. "Charley, take my car. Go ask Bob Franklin if we can use his boat."

Grateful that somebody else was assuming command, Nathan clambered into the Ford. "I'd better bring back a sheet," he said, "to cover the body."

"Good idea." Ordinarily, the newsman would have winced as he watched his new car tear away, leaving a solid wall of dust in its wake, but not today. He was enjoying himself too much.

Franklin's Trailer Court was two blocks away, which meant that Charley could return with the motor-powered dinghy within twenty minutes. "Relax, Ed," Sam said. "There's not much we can do 'til he gets back. And that stiff's not going anywhere."

A mild breeze was blowing across the lake, cooling the air and making Jackson wished he'd brought his jacket. "So, what the hell's going on?" he asked.

"I really don't know, Sam. Len Hackman was dusting his crops this morning. He was playing dive bomber over the lake, and spotted this body floating face up. With clothes on. He phoned it in. That's all there is to tell."

"With *clothes* on!?!"

"That's what they told me." LaGrange anticipated Sam's next remark. "I know. That's what I thought. "Why would somebody go swimming with their clothes on?"

"Maybe you don't have a drowning out there," mused Jackson. "You ever hear of anybody drowning in Mineral Lake?"

Mineral Lake was a freak of nature: a three-mile-long body of water containing twenty-seven different inorganic substances, which, according to doctors, were effective in treatment of arthritis and rheumatism. Victims of these diseases flocked to the mild desert resort on the lake's south shore every summer to bathe in the soapy-like, pain-easing waters. Retirees often became permanent residents. The minerals made the lake dense and buoyant. To sink beneath its surface was almost impossible.

Now that he'd raised the point, Sam even recalled that summer before last, a swimmer with a leg cramp had stayed afloat over twenty minutes until help arrived.

"He could have had a heart attack," tendered the deputy, anxiously glancing toward the white-cap dotted water.

"That doesn't explain the clothes," replied Sam. "It might not be a bad idea if you alerted the State Police."

He was sure of one thing. Arlene would be walking home from church today.

LaGrange was cutting the lock off Barnett's gate with a hacksaw supplied by a nearby resident when Nathan returned with more than the dinghy in tow.

"What's that goddamn battle-ax doing here?" Jackson pondered aloud, taken aback at seeing the 260-pound bulk of Mayor Maggie Murphy occupying the passenger side of his Ford, and her bespectacled wimpy son, Sean, in the back seat.

Nathan, embarrassed, opened the door for the town's white-haired chief executive. "'I'm sorry, Sam," he whispered. "She showed up while I was hitching up the boat. Insisted on coming down here."

"Fine," replied Jackson. "You amuse her while Ed and I do what has to be done."

Tossing his stogie down on the sand, he stalked over to the fence and stared out at the water. He knew damn well that Nathan was relieved that bitch was here. She was theoretically in charge now. The responsibility was off Charley's back. Hell, knowing him, he probably called her and asked her to join them.

Sam didn't like people who played dictator, and Maggie Murphy was one of those people. She'd been mayor for over fifteen years, running the town as if she owned it, which, in a sense, she did. At least 35 percent of it, including a deteriorating hotel built by her father back in 1917.

Maggie's cronies and the people who either worked or rented from her kept the widow in office. Her power had prevented Mineral Lake from blossoming into its full potential as a resort. Why should she encourage new money to come in; give her competition by building a first-class hotel, good restaurants and nice shops? This was her town and nobody was going to do anything to change it.

Perhaps what bothered Jackson most was his own reluctance to publicly challenge her authority. Maggie knew he despised her. That was all right, so long as he didn't use his paper as a tool to oppose her. How could he? If she wanted to use it, she had enough clout to see that he lost eighty percent of his advertising and printing customers. The truce between them was about as stable as that between North and South Korea.

Mother and son were quite a sight to behold. The massive sixty-five-year-old Maggie was waddling down to the fence in her tent-sized print dress, grunting at friends in the crowd.

Sean, a prissy beanpole with pencil-thin mustache, trailing after. The 30-year-old "lad," whose standard attire included white shirt and tie, was seldom seen without his mother, always following a respectful two steps behind her.

"What was he doing out there in the first place?" the mayor demanded as LaGrange struggled with the hacksaw.

Not quite sure how he should respond, Ed glanced at Jackson, who pretended to ignore him. "We don't know that yet, Mrs. Mayor."

"I hope we can keep this a local matter. Bad publicity to have a drowning here."

Again LaGrange looked toward Sam for assistance and the editor acquiesced. "Mrs. Mayor," he began, his expression that of a man who's just drawn his fourth ace, "I'm sorry, but we've already sent for the State Police."

He loved it when Maggie got angry. Her face turned crimson, and for several seconds she could only sputter. "Why...Why wasn't I consulted first?" she blurted finally. "Are you trying to destroy this town?"

Sam maintained his cool, sauntering over, catching the odor of cheap bourbon that was always on her breath. "It appears that we have a 'death under mysterious circumstances' here, he said quietly. "The town sheriff is not equipped to handle it. It's as simple as that."

"Oscar Heath is perfectly capable...."

"He's gone fishing, lady!" shouted Jackson. "And Ed here is nothing more than a traffic cop. What do you want? A formal inquiry into how you screwed up the investigation into some poor bastard's death?"

"Well, get on with it," the mayor said testily. "That damn Barnett!" Sam heard her announce to someone. "If that rotten fence wasn't there, they'd have been out in the water by now. I ought to pass an ordinance and have it torn down."

Sam was amused. If it hadn't been for her calling Harry Barnett a "damn *kike*" when he'd disagreed with her at a city council meeting last July, that fence wouldn't be there, and the lake's only naturally sandy beach would still be open to the public free of charge.

It had been a stupid thing for Maggie to say, like biting the hand that feeds you.

The vast majority of Mineral Lake's summer visitors were Jews. Most of them came from Seattle, a four-hour drive away. The money these families spent here each year served as the backbone of the town's economy.

Some of the local businesses and motel owners may have resented being so dependent on "God's chosen people," but most were wise enough to set their personal prejudices aside during the summer months. They knew how to smile and make these tourists feel welcome.

But then, Harry Barnett was not your typical tourist.

Barnett liked this town, believed in its potential, and even owned a large vacation house here. Nevertheless, right after that stormy council meeting, he and his family had returned home to Seattle. He'd told the motel operators who were afraid of losing their tourist trade that the fence would come down only after they'd voted in a new mayor.

Jackson admired Harry Barnett, as did many of the town's more progressive-minded citizens. The wealthy jeweler was an obstinate son-of-a-bitch, but the only one with balls enough to fight that Irish anachronism head-on. With some luck, and much clandestine maneuvering, it was quite possible that Mrs. Murphy would be retiring from public life after the next election.

"Got it!" said LaGrange, as he snapped off the lock and swung open the gate. "Let's get that boat launched." He turned to the newspaperman. "Wanna come?"

Jackson didn't feel too comfortable going out onto the lake in a ten-foot dinghy. The breeze had become stronger, making the surface choppy, and the boat's small outboard was barely strong enough to propel the craft, let alone its two occupants.

Perhaps they should have waited for the State Police. They, after all, were better trained and equipped to retrieve a body. But, with them, there would come reporters from neighboring towns. Sam was determined that the first break on this story, be it foul play or just a simple drowning, was going to be his exclusively.

LaGrange, who was sitting up front with the binoculars, directed him to steer to the right. "It's drifted around the bluff," he shouted, trying to make himself heard over the erratic sound of the motor.

The editor maneuvered a wide course around the fifty-foot high stack of black boulders jutting out from the shoreline. The chances of piling-up on these rocks were quite slim. What he was trying to avoid was the unbearable stench emitted from the pools of black, sulfurous mud on top of the palisade.

The derelict bath house on the cliff stared down at them. Its charred stone walls were the only remnants of the fashionable therapeutic center destroyed by fire long before Sam had even heard of Mineral Lake. People used to come here during the twenties and bathe in that stinking goo, but, now, the mud was brought down into the town spas.

Glancing back toward the beach, Sam saw that the number of spectators had increased, and the ambulance from the hospital had arrived. Still no State Police cars. If his luck held, he might even be able to get back to his office and phone the story into the Spokane wire services before any other papers got wind of it. If there was a story, that is.

"Over there," yelled LaGrange.

Sam saw the corpse now. It was floating on its back about ten yards off to the right. As the boat chugged closer, he could distinguish the bobbing figure of a man, dressed in dark coveralls and the strips of what was once a plaid shirt.

"Who is it?" he asked the deputy.

"My God!" gasped Ed, turning his face away. "What the hell happened to him?"

The boat pulled up next to the remains, giving Jackson a good view. It was like nothing he had ever seen during his days as a police reporter. He felt like vomiting.

The body, covered with a thin layer of lake scum, appeared to be bleached white, as if all the blood had been drained from it. What looked like deep claw marks stretched diagonally across the face, making it unrecognizable. The right eye was dangling from its socket.

Cause of death appeared obvious to the newsman. The man's throat had been torn open and his jugular vein apparently ripped out.

LaGrange looked at the older man. "Who could have done this?" he asked, not wanting to believe what he had seen.

"You mean, *what*," corrected Sam, staring out across the lake. "What could have done this?"

ONE

1974

    "When are we going to be there, Daddy?" The five-year-old must have asked Jay Barnett that question 20 times since they'd left Seattle over two hours ago.

    "Another 45 minutes, Dave."

    "How long is that?"

    Games of abstracts were a regular routine between father and son these days when they were together. Jay answered, "Figure almost as long as 'Sesame Street'."

    "Aw, Dad," the round-featured boy replied. "I want to be there now."

    Despite feeling cramped behind the wheel of the new yellow Skylark he'd rented, Jay was finding the drive a pleasant one, traveling through the majestic snowcapped Cascade Mountains, across the tranquil farmlands of Central Washington. This was scenery he hadn't seen since he was 15, all of 16 years ago. The route was an hour faster now, almost total freeway, which meant that many of the small speed-trap towns along the way were skirted.

    "How about some music, Daver?" he suggested, turning on the car radio. Static. They were too far away from a strong radio signal, and the surrounding mountains made listening to what did filter through a chore. Fiddling with the dial, he caught a snatch of news about Watergate and President Nixon's impending resignation, and couldn't help wondering how "Tricky Dick" was going to pull himself out of this one. Then, tired of the interference, switched the radio off.

Jay scratched at his closely cropped, slightly graying beard. The August sun in this barren, though stunning, temperate desert region made the damn thing itchy and uncomfortable. He wasn't going to give into the temptation, though, and shave it off. It added too much style to his appearance, and, besides, the ladies he was dating liked it. The growth also offset the fact that he was still a little overweight.

What was it that Helen said right about the time they'd decided to divorce last year? "You're only growing a beard because you want to change your life style."

Maybe she was right.

Naw, she was only partially correct. The truth was that he hated shaving. Pre-beard, he would pace around the house for thirty minutes every morning, trying to delay the inevitable act of running that nasty safety razor over his face.

The truth was that he was lazy…except when it came to his writing.

"You come home from work," Helen would complain. "You go into your office…and you sit at that goddamn typewriter half the night. What kind of marriage is that?"

"I'm writing," Jay'd retort. "I make money from my writing…and you like to spend that money."

That, like everything else, was just part of the truth. Writing was also an excuse to avoid Helen, her drinking and her constant badgering. He was doing what he wanted to do, and he didn't want to deal with her complaints…no matter how legitimate they might or might not be.

The final straw had been broken the night that she, once again, had had one too many drinks, and announced, "I hate your writing and I think you're a lousy writer."

The remark had cut Jay to the bone. It was midnight, yet he'd still packed a bag and left the house. For him, the marriage was over.

Periodically, he pondered his failed relationship with Helen. If he'd been home more…paid more attention to her…would she have drunk as much as she did?

These moments of self-analysis never lasted very long. There were always other, less painful, subjects to think about.

Ever restless, David, in tattered cut-offs and a Superman T-shirt, climbed over into the back seat again and stared out the rear window. "Want to sing some Disney songs, Dave?" Jay asked.

"*Nawh.*"

"How about some riddles?"

"No way."

"Well, what would you like to do?"

"Go home."

The little *shit* really knew how to stick him where it hurt, just like his mother. Jay had been planning the Seattle vacation for the two of them for over six months. It would be the first extended period of time father and son would have together since the split. Dave had been excited at the prospect of meeting uncles, aunts and cousins he'd only heard about.

During the past ten days, they'd both enjoyed themselves, become close again. They'd stayed with Jay's younger brother, Alan, and his family on Mercer Island, viewed the old family home on Capitol Hill, and ran and roughhoused amid the evergreen trees in the city's well-kept Volunteer Park. Dave seemed to enjoy his father's recounting of youthful adventures that accompanied tours back to his elementary and high schools. But every time Barnett asked the child to do something he didn't want to do, he struck back by saying he wanted to go home.

Jay was aware that these remarks were only Dave's anger at the divorce itself. The knowledge didn't make them any less painful. Maybe this side trip to the old Barnett summer home would amuse Daver.

He'd certainly told him enough stories about the place, concentrating on the scattered moments of fun he'd had there when he was a little boy, rather than the reality that the town was no Disneyland.

Jay was hopeful that his son would enjoy Mineral Lake. He wanted Dave to have a vacation to remember.

The Skylark glided over the green steel girder bridge that crossed the Columbia River at Vantage. They drove up the road carved into the canyon wall beyond. "Hey, Daver," Jay said, checking his watch. "Want to stop for a few minutes and see something pretty?" There was still two hours before his one-thirty business meeting, and he needed to stretch his legs.

"Okay."

"This is going to look like something right out of a cowboy movie," Jay announced as he stopped the car at the canyon's rim. With Jay holding his son's hand, they walked a few feet up the highway to a point where they could stare down into the wide gorge, and the blue river rushing through it half a mile below.

"I'll bet a hundred years ago Indians rode along these canyons," Jay said, pointing to rust-colored cliffs on the other side. Ever since his early teens, he'd wondered why Hollywood had never discovered this magnificent country. It was a perfect background for Westerns and, if he ever got another one of his own film projects off the ground, he planned to make good use of it.

"Did John Wayne shoot Indians here?"

"Well, somebody like him maybe did. John Wayne's just an actor, Dave. The movies are just pretend." He was continually telling his son that movies were not real.

Barnett was proud of his sandy-haired little son, a bright, well-built, feisty kid, certainly destined to top Jay's 5'8" by at least another half-foot. Unlike his father, Dave was a physical person. He was a good athlete, already playing pee wee soccer back home. The team coach considered him one of his best defensive players.

"So, what do you think, tiger?" Jay asked, unbuttoning his shirt and squatting next to the child. "Isn't this great country?"

"Uh-huh." Without warning, Dave put his arms around his father's neck and kissed him on the cheek. "Dad, I'm sorry I said I wanted to go home. I really want to be with you."

"I know you do, son," Jay said warmly. "I like being with you, too."

They hugged for a moment, then hand in hand walked back to the car.

"Can we go swimming in the lake?" the boy asked, as the auto moved along flat terrain now.

"I don't think we're going to have time, Dave," Jay said. "My meeting is probably going to take an hour or so and, then, I wanted to try and look up my friend, Jerry. You remember, I told you about him."

"The man with the porcupine?"

"Something like that," Jay said. He was getting slightly weary, not really in the mood to relate the porcupine saga again for the fiftieth or so time: of how he and Jerry at the age of 12 had bagged a wild porcupine that had wandered into the outskirts of Mineral Lake, then had constructed a makeshift cage from which the animal had easily escaped. There had sure been a lot of dogs yelping in pain the night ol' Porky decided to take it on the lam.

Jerry Roscoe was one of the few kids Jay had really got to know during his lazy summers at the lake. He was a permanent resident and about the only local kid who didn't resent the 'rich Jew boy' that spent ten weeks each year in the staid resort town. They were inseparable buddies -- with Jay in the lead -- swimming, hiking, but, mostly, just goofing around.

Watching the empty two-lane road stretch before him, Jay thought of Carol. She was another regular summer visitor. She stayed with her grandparents, the Franklins, at their trailer court.

He'd lost his virginity to Carol at age 15. That long auburn hair and her warm maturing breasts beneath the maroon mini-halter she always wore were just too much of a turn-on for him to resist the night they went swimming on his folk's empty beach.

Funny how one never forgets his first sexual experience.

What had become of her? Probably she was home in Yakima, married to a farmer, and with a house filled with kids.

"Can't we go swimming tomorrow?" Dave asked, interrupting his father's journey into nostalgia. "I'll be okay, Dad. You said that nobody can drown in the lake."

"Let's see what happens, tiger. You know we're due back in Seattle tomorrow night for dinner with Uncle Don and Aunt Sarah."

"Ah, come on, Dad. Please!"

"I'll try to work it out, Dave. Okay?" In spite of his sentimental mood, Jay wanted to head back to Seattle right after breakfast. If Mineral Lake was anything like he remembered it, the town would be boredom incarnate. Certainly it was no place to stay for more than 24 hours. But, if it would make Dave happy, perhaps they could take a dip sometime before they took off.

"Look over there, son," he said, pointing with a tinge of recognition to a spot some three miles in the distance. "We're there. Those cliffs over there. Just below them is the lake."

The pole-lined route seemed strangely unchanged to Jay after 16 years. Roadsides during the earlier part of his journey were modern, beautified with well-kept trees and shrubs. Here, outside Mineral Lake, they appeared almost frozen in time. He saw the same decaying empty shacks and fruit stands, uncontrolled sagebrush, and felt the same aura of total desolation he remembered from his teens. He wondered why the city fathers were so indifferent to the main entrance into their resort, especially since the Grand Coulee Dam via the Columbia Basin Project provided ample irrigation water to the area.

Jay, at first, gave little thought to the man walking in the distance along the right side of the road. As he closed the gap, however, he saw the spindliness of the figure. His toothpick legs were thrust out of frayed oversized shorts. Sandals, a drooping soiled undershirt, a flat white cap and a knapsack completed the elder's quite functional attire.

Something was definitely familiar about this old codger, mused Barnett as they passed him. But what it was, he didn't know. He looked like so many of the retirees who lived in and around Mineral Lake that, perhaps, Jay was reacting to the specific type.

A casual glance at the rear-view mirror and he remembered. "Hell," Jay said to himself, "I thought he was dead!"

Childhood memories poured forth. He'd been a little older than Dave when this senior citizen, who must have been pushing 60 even then, had begun working for his parents, maintaining the grounds of the family summer estate. He called himself "the Storyman," claiming that, as a boy, he'd traveled with the Buffalo Bill Circus. Nobody knew if that was a fable or not, nor did many really care. The gardener was a virtual Pied Piper. Children tagged after him, listening to the multitude of tales he relished relating to any tyke who would sit at his feet with eyes wide and mouth agape.

Jay had always kidded his mother about the utter panic she'd experienced when the Storyman had first appeared on the scene. After all, reasoned Mama, who was to know if the man was a pervert or not? While Jay and other kids were on the beach being enthralled with tales of Paul Bunyan and Jesse James, she would sit nervously on the front porch, studying every action through a pair of binoculars.

Barnett turned the vehicle onto the shoulder and shut off the engine. "Dave," he said, opening the door. "Wait here for a minute. I want to talk to that man."

"I want to go, too."

"Stay here. If he's who I think he is, I'll bring him back to the car."

What was his real name? He tried to recall. "O'Reilly? O'Hara? O'Neil! That was it. Albert O'Neil.

He was a lonely old soul, Jay remembered; divorced and with a daughter he hadn't seen in years. No wonder he loved kids.

"Mr. O'Neil? How are you?" Jay extended his hand. "I'm Harry Barnett's son, Jay. It's been a long time."

The man squinted at him through his wire-framed glasses, no hint of recognition on his wizened visage. "Who'd you say you were?"

"Jay Barnett. You used to take care of my folks' place 15 or 20 years ago. When I was little, you told me stories."

"I used to tell a lot of children stories." O'Neil took a grimy handkerchief out of a back pocket to wipe the sweat from his wrinkles. "Thousands of kids."

"I was one of your biggest fans," Jay said with a wide grin.

"Problem is that the children get older, nine or ten, and they forget. They don't have time for stories anymore. Funny, I can remember the faces of the little ones, but when they grow up...."

O'Neil studied the younger man's features, reaching into the depths of his dwindling memory in an effort to recall the relationship. "You say you knew Harry Barnett?"

"He was my father," Jay repeated patiently. "I came here every summer until I was 15"

"Oh, you're Harry's boy," O'Neil said in a tone that made Jay wonder if he had truly recognized him. "You've gotten older."

"Haven't we all?'

"I'm 85-years-old now," the Storyman announced with pride. 'Still walk into town every day...do some weeding...."

"Can I give you a ride? It's a pretty hot day to be walking."

"I haven't seen Harry for a while," the oldster said, as they walked back to the Skylark.

"My parents passed away. Dad died over eight years ago."

"Wondered why he hadn't been around."

"Hey, Daver," Jay said as he opened the car door for O'Neil. The boy stopped bouncing up and down on the seat. "I want you to meet somebody. Remember the stories I told you about the Storyman?" Dave nodded. "Well, this is him. Mr. O'Neil, this is my son, David."

"Hello, youngster," O'Neil said with a spark of interest. "How old are you?"

Jay could see his old friend felt more comfortable now that he had a child with whom he could relate. As he walked around to the driver's side, he watched the pair getting acquainted and thought that it would be nice if the boy were able to spend some time with the Storyman, experience the wonderment of his tales, tall and true.

"Do you still tell stories?" Barnett asked, steering the car back onto the highway.

"There's not many kids around to listen anymore."

"Would you tell me a story?" David piped up.

"I sure would, if it's okay with your dad."

"Maybe later today, or tomorrow morning before we leave. We could stop off at your place, if that's convenient. You still out off the highway?"

"Same place for all these years. You're both welcome anytime."

"We'll try to make it in the morning."

O'Neil beamed, turned and smiled at the boy. Where do you folks live these days? Seattle?"

"Los Angeles," Jay answered. "L.A. County, that is. I'm actually in a suburb called Tarzana."

"How come you live all the way down there?"

"I'm in the entertainment business."

"Entertainment business?"

"Yeah, I've got my own public relations firm, I write books about Hollywood and I just finished making my first movie."

"That's real nice," commented O'Neil, still looking at David. "You back here for a vacation?"

"Mostly business. A gentleman from Spokane is buying the last of the Barnett real estate, a three-acre lot, and I'm here to meet him, sign some papers and pick up a check. That's all. I've got to be back in L.A. early next week."

They were inside the city limits now. Jay spotted the one-story rambling Mason Hospital to his left, its sprinkler system going full tilt.

Across the way stood the Foodland market where his mother once shopped and he and Jerry Roscoe would buy at least two popsicles a day. Its broken windows were boarded up and graffiti marred the walls.

"Tell me, Mr. O'Neil," Jay said. "Do you remember a boy about my age, Jerry Roscoe? His father owned a tavern in town.

Again, the old man poked about in his memories. "There were so many of you kids. What'd he look like?

"He was just a normal kid. We were together all the time. I think his father's place was called the 'Red Robin Tavern'."

"Did he have real light blond hair, almost white?"

"That's him. He still live here?"

"Nope." The Storyman paused for a second. "He's dead."

Startled by the news, Barnett looked to the octogenarian for elaboration.

"He were killed a long time ago," continued O'Neil. "He were burned to a crisp."

TWO

Barnett sat at the curb for nearly five minutes after he dropped off the Storyman. Ignoring his son's "Let's go!" and "Get a move on, Dad," he tried to recall a single characteristic of the Jerry Roscoe he'd known 16 years ago that would justify the behavior of the adult that O'Neil had described.

"He just turned bad," the oldster proclaimed. "He were always drunk or on them dope pills kids take nowadays."

It was hard to conceive of Jerry taking drugs. As Jay remembered him, he was just an ordinary kid; quiet, introspective, with no particular hang-ups.

While Jerry's father was in Korea, his mother had taken charge of the family tavern, then after he'd been blown to bits there, she just kept on running it. Her mother, Grandma Flowers, they called her, had moved from somewhere in Wyoming to run the house and Jerry.

Despite the absence of his father, Jerry seemed to have a healthy relationship with his mother and grandmother. They were god people, a nice family.

On the other hand, he was a born follower. Jerry had seldom taken the initiative on anything. He'd almost always gone along with whatever Jay wanted. Like the night they decided to relieve their boredom by letting the air out of the tires of all the cars parked on First Street. It had been Jay's idea, and after a mild objection, Jerry had participated with equal gusto.

No, if Jerry Roscoe had experimented with drugs, somebody he'd admired had pointed the way.

Jay found O'Neil's vaguely remembered description of the accident chilling.

"He were up on the cliffs above the lake," the old man had said, "in that speed car of his. And he went over. Crashed smack in the middle of the highway. The car just exploded."

It was difficult for Jay to feel any deep emotional response at Jerry's passing. There was a definite disappointment now that the anticipated reunion was impossible, but then he hadn't seen Jerry for years. What more could be expected?

Hell, he didn't even cry when his parents died, even though he felt he should have. It was easier for him to hold it inside, to intellectualize his feelings away. Life was much smoother when one just avoided its more painful aspects.

"Dad," David said, shaking Jay's shoulder, "would you wake up so we can go?"

Barnett's first notion, turning east onto Main Street, was that Mineral Lake had shrunk in size. It was much smaller than he recalled, and considerably quieter. Not that the town was ever a vacationer's paradise, but years ago, streets during August had a fair amount of tourist traffic. People dropped in and out of the local souvenir shops or relaxed on the porches of the various dreary hotels. Now, only a half-dozen elderly folk were to be seen, and they were probably locals.

No new commercial structures had been built since he'd been here so long ago, and about forty percent of the existing storefronts had a "For Rent" sign in the window. Gone were the gift shops, the dry goods store, and the newsstand where he'd spend most of his weekly allowance buying comic books and, later, Hollywood fan magazines.

Even the local movie house was boarded up and stripped of exterior fixtures.

Jay was always saddened when a theater went out of business. He'd received so many hours of solace and pleasure in those dark places.

The print shop was still at the same old stand, a discovery which made Barnett happy. He had liked the owner, Sam Jackson, and wondered if he still ran the business. Probably not, since the old *Mineral Lake Bulletin* sign was no longer above the door.

Taverns, rest homes and health spas featuring therapeutic massage and mud baths were the most flourishing kinds of businesses on Main, though Jay did note that the drug store was still there, without its once-crowded soda fountain. So were Al's cafe and the Mineral Lake Grill, two joints usually frequented in past years by locals, rather than tourists.

He was glad his father wasn't around to see the deterioration. After putting so much time, money and heart into the resort, Harry would have found its present condition unbearable.

He wondered what had happened here. What had killed the town?

"Where'd you use to live, Dad?" asked Dave, unimpressed with the storyland he'd heard so much about.

"It's on the other side of town. We'll take a look at it after my meeting."

"Aw, Dad...."

"Come on, tiger. It's almost one-thirty. I don't want to be late."

"Why'd we have to come to this dumb ol' place anyway?"

Jay didn't think it necessary to answer. He certainly had to agree with the sentiments.

He pulled into a diagonal parking space in front of the Washington National Bank, still sharing a one-story brick structure with an attorney's office.

"Dad, I wanna play on the swings," said Dave, darting out into the street as his father removed his attaché´ case from the trunk.

"Hey!" Jay bounded after the boy and grabbed his hand. "You know better than that. You don't cross the street without me. Remember?"

"I wanna play on the swings," Dave insisted.

"What swings?"

"The ones over there." The boy pointed to the Murphy Hotel across the way where a children's play yard sat empty. In it were a weather-worn swing and slide set and a sandbox. The Murphy, a faded orange stucco two-story building, looked as abandoned as its play yard.

"I don't know if you should, Daver. I think that's private property."

"What's private property?"

A blue Chevy van had slowed to a stop while father and son were negotiating in the middle of the street. Jay smiled an apology to the driver, whose face was obscured by the sun's reflection on the windshield. He led his protesting youngster over to the curb. "Let me ask inside the bank," Jay said, realizing he'd never find a better baby sitter than the play yard. "Maybe it'll be okay."

They entered the building into a welcome cold blast from an overactive air conditioning system.

Jay was sure that this antiquated branch of the Washington National had been designed in the days of John Dillinger and Bonnie and Clyde. With its two inhospitable teller cages, separating employees from customers by steel bars, and a middle-aged, uniformed security guard sitting in the corner reading the *National Enquirer*, it looked like a 1930s movie set.

He sat David on a bench by the window, then crossed the checkerboard linoleum floor to the first cage. "Good afternoon," he said to the matronly teller.

Adjusting her bifocals, she glanced up from the back of a deposit slip, her thin lips betraying no hint of a smile.

"Is Mr. Parish in?"

"Who should I say is calling?" she asked formally, trying to avoid staring at his beard. It was strange how, in this part of the country, hair on the face made you an automatic suspect.

"Jay Barnett."

"Oh, Mr. Barnett. He's expecting you." Still no attempt to be friendly. She excused herself and walked with short brisk steps to a wooden door in the rear, marked "Private."

"How you doin', Daver?" Barnett called to his son, who was peering under the bench.

"Dad, ask about the swings!"

"I'll ask, I'll ask."

The woman returned from the back office, followed by a delicate little man with horn-rimmed glasses and a receding hairline. According to Jay's type-casting, he could be no less than the bank manager. Who else on a scorching day like this would wear a long-sleeved dress shirt and dark business suit?

The official approached Jay with hand extended, his eyes only momentarily betraying his disapproval of the out-of-towner's beard. "Mr. Barnett," he said. "I'm John Parish. It's a pleasure to know you." His handshake was firm, not what Jay had expected from such a slight, prissy person. "We tried to call you this morning, but you'd already left Seattle."

"What's the problem?"

"I'm truly sorry for any inconvenience this might cause you, but we did try to reach you just as soon as we heard."

"What's happened?" asked Jay.

"Nothing irreparable. It's just that Mr. Gousha, the gentleman from Spokane, can't be here until Monday morning."

Jay could feel his father's rabid temper rising within him. "Why the hell not?" he demanded, just as Harry would have done.

"There's been a death in his family. His sister. The funeral is Sunday, and he'll be here when we open Monday morning."

"That's just great!" Jay growled, beginning to pace the floor. "I'm sorry his sister died, but his is Thursday!"

"What's the matter, Dad?" Dave asked?

"We're stuck here all weekend, tiger. That's all."

"Really, Mr. Barnett," Parish said, "we did try to call you at your brother's house. He said you'd left about fifteen minutes before."

"Hey, I gotta get back to Seattle tomorrow," Jay pleaded. "I'm due in L.A. on Monday."

"I really wish there was something I could do. Perhaps your arrangements could be consummated through the mails?"

"No. I need that twenty-five thousand in my hand by the first of the week. I've got a film that I've got to get out of the lab."

"I beg your pardon?" Parish said.

"I made a low-budget movie. Tied up all my money in it. The lab took a deferment, and now they want their cash."

"You tied up *all* your funds in a motion picture? That's rather risky, isn't it?""

Jay resented Parish's sudden surge of superiority. "Probably," he said, "but if the gentleman from Spokane had closed the deal two months ago and had not been jerking me around, I wouldn't have this problem now."

30

"Mr. Gousha said he'd have the papers ready for signature and a cashier's check made out to you on Monday morning."

From Parish's tone, Jay knew that was that. There was no sense in arguing, even if it did make him feel better. If he didn't want to lose his film, he was stuck for the weekend.

Going back to Seattle now would be a dumb idea. Better to re-adjust his schedule. He'd been rushing around too much already on this vacation, giving David the grand tour and plugging his new book on Clark Gable with the Seattle press so he'd be able to write off the entire trip as business. Perhaps this layover was a blessing in disguise. He might be bored, but at least he could relax for a couple of days and spend the time with David.

"May I use your phone?" he asked Parish. "I have to cancel my plans for tomorrow and also see if I can get a late flight back to Los Angeles Monday night. I'll have the operator charge the calls to my home."

"Please come into my office."

"Come on, Dave" Jay motioned to his son.

"Dad...*the swings!*"

"I'm only going to be five minutes, Tiger. I've got to call your Uncle Alan, then we'll leave."

"Dad...!"

Parish's office was furnished with a blond wooden desk and straight chairs of 1940s' design. They were badly in need of refinishing. Two color portraits adorned the buff walls, Generals Dwight D. Eisenhower and Douglas MacArthur, both in full uniform.

The manager invited Jay to be seated, then passed the phone over the desk to him. "Want to look at a picture book, sonny?" he said to David, who was gazing out the window at a refuse area behind the building.

"What kind of pictures?"

"Pictures of soldiers." He handed Dave a large volume, entitled *A Pictorial History of the Pacific War*. "Now, be careful with it."

"Are you a student of military history?" Jay asked casually, waiting for the operator to come on line.

"I find it a fascinating subject. Why, the logistics of battle are like a championship chess match, only far more complex."

"I'll bet you saw *Patton* ten times."

"Only three," the manager beamed. "I drove all the way to Spokane to see it the first time. It was a great movie."

Somehow, Jay thought, Parish didn't seem like the type to be a military aficionado, but his first impressions had been wrong before. When that shapely brunette had walked into his Hollywood publicity office, for instance. He had been about to ask her for a date when she announced she was a transsexual and, like sex change recipient Christine Jorgensen had done in the 1950s, she wanted to be promoted into an international celebrity.

The call to his brother took less than three minutes. Alan assured Jay that he would make apologies to the family and switch his plane reservations. Both were sorry the visit was to be cut short, however 25 thousand was a lot of money.

"Can you suggest a good motel?" Barnett asked the manager as he and Dave were leaving.

"There's the Royal Inn on the west side," replied Parish. "They take the major credit cards. Or, Murphy's. Right across the street. It's an old hotel, but quite reasonable."

Jay laughed. "Mr. Parish, if I even walked into Murphy's, my father would turn over in his grave."

"That's right," the banker chuckled, embarrassed. "I've heard about the altercation he had with Maggie. It's almost folklore around here."

"My dad closed our beach to the town for two years until she was voted out of office. Is she still alive?"

"Yes, and as cantankerous as ever, though she has some trouble getting around these days. Her son, Sean, pretty much looks after her affairs now."

The trio was on the sidewalk and, once again, Jay noticed the empty storefronts. "What happened to this town, Mr. Parish?" When I last saw it 16 years ago, it was a thriving resort."

"It isn't much different from when I was transferred here two years ago." The manager seemed reluctant to continue. "Most of the stores were like you see them. What we need is a first class hotel to attract visitors. But nobody's going to finance one until the tourist trade picks up by itself. It's a vicious circle."

"Why'd people stop coming here?"

Again Parish avoided a direct answer. "Did you know Sam Jackson? He runs the print shop."

Jay nodded.

"Ask him. He used to publish the local newspaper. He's also the self-appointed town historian."

The blue Chevy van, parked in the alley next to the bank, waited until Barnett's yellow Skylark was well on its way down the street before it fell in behind, maintaining a distance of one block.

Jay felt a flush of excitement as they traveled west on Main toward the Royal Inn. Their route would take them past the family's old summer estate. He was anxious to see if the house and grounds had weathered the years better than the rest of the town. Most likely they would have escaped the malady that had blighted Mineral Lake. The property had been bought eight years ago by a respected attorney.

He was not disappointed. The house, with its outer walls of black granite boulder and green asphalt roof, was just as he'd remembered it, as was the large, well-tended lawn with its fruit trees. Situated on the highest corner of the undeveloped multi-acre lot separating the west beach from Main, the one-time showplace enjoyed a commanding view of the entire lake and surrounding cliffs. Harry Barnett had built it for 20 thousand dollars in the late 1940s.

"Here it is, tiger." Jay stopped the Skylark in front of the house. "This is where your Uncle Alan and I spent our summers when we were kids."

"Where's the merry-go-round?" Dave asked.

"That was sold years ago." Jay was amused at how the boy consistently remembered stories he'd mentioned only in passing, like the porcupine saga, or the tale of the merry-go-round.

Harry Barnett had always done things designed to raise a few eyebrows. One summer, he'd paid one thousand dollars for a small carnival, including a merry-go-round, he'd discovered stalled on the side of the highway. Harry knew nothing about the amusement business, but with his money he could afford to buy an expensive "toy" like this for his kids, and himself.

Jay reveled in his few happy memories of Mineral Lake. More common were the disturbing recollections, of an over-protective mother and an often domineering father who never really tried to know his older, more intellectual son. The elder Barnett was not a cruel man, but one of little patience. Unfortunately, he was fifty-five when Jay was born. They'd never been close; never had the kind of relationship where either father or son felt he could reach out and touch the other with affection. Neither of them had ever learned how.

How often an initially peaceful discussion ended with Harry's utilizing a belt or even a baseball bat to win his point, Jay couldn't begin to remember. When he was 16, the crazy old bastard had even come after him with a gun.

More than once, he was saved from this father's wrath by Mama's threats to have her husband arrested for child beating. And, wasn't it odd how that prospect upset Jay more than the promised whipping.

The late patriarch's insensitivity had cursed his son in another, more lasting way. From childhood, Jay had been frightened of pain to the point where he would shrink from any confrontation that might result in violence. Thus, he'd developed a quick gift of gab, and had bluffed himself out of several tight situations. The prowess also served him well in his business.

Nine months with an analyst had made him cognizant of the reasons why he became weak and fearful when the words wouldn't work and he was forced to face a physical threat, real or imaginary. Daddy's years of conditioning had ingrained the behavior pattern too deeply to change him emotionally.

Certainly that's why Jay, though he'd inherited his father's quick temper, hated to spank his own child, even when he justly deserved it. That was why, too, Dave was well on his way to becoming a spoiled brat.

"Can we go in the house?" Dave asked.

"Maybe. Let's check into the motel, then come back here and talk to the owners."

The few other houses along the blacktopped street had not fared as well as the old homestead. Those that didn't have "For Sale" signs imbedded in their dying front lawns were accented by peeling paint and dangling shingles. Most of the town seemed to have simply surrendered to the elements.

Two blocks from his former summer retreat, they drove past the Franklin Trailer Court. It boasted a lush green lawn and a row of freshly painted guest cottages; an oasis in a wasteland.

As Jay recalled, the place had always been well cared for. Mr. Franklin, the original owner, had been that kind of innkeeper, always going to extra pains to make his guests comfortable. He'd been very friendly to Jay; had taken him and Jerry fishing a few times at nearby Blue Lake. He'd even encouraged the teenager to spend time with his visiting granddaughter, Carol. Not that Jay had needed any encouragement.

Jay had been truly saddened five years ago to hear that the old man had died of a stroke.

Who the hell was running the place now? "Hey, Dave, how'd you like to stay here instead of the other place we were going?"

"How come?" The boy didn't seem to care one way or another.

"It used to belong to a friend of mine. Besides, we'll only be two blocks from the beach."

"Goodie! Can we go swimming today?"

"We'll see."

Jay parked on the gravel drive in front of the small wood frame house that also served as an office. With only nine of the twenty house trailer spaces filled, the court was considerably emptier than in past years, though a few of the cottages seemed to have guests occupying them.

The blue Chevy van passed by the court entrance without pausing, and continued down Main.

A man of Jay's age opened the screen door of the house. A husky fellow, he probably would have been a football player if it wasn't that his left pant leg was empty and pinned up. "How are ya?" He rested on his crutches, sipping from a glass filled with a dark liquid that smelled like cheap bourbon. "Lookin' for a place to stay?"

"Until Monday morning," replied Jay. He noticed Dave staring at their host's sole leg and said a silent prayer that the boy wouldn't ask his inevitable question aloud. "Tiger, why don't you go play over there on the lawn until I finish registering." He pointed across the driveway to a green, tree-lined area with wicker furniture.

"Uh-uh."

"Go!!" Jay ordered, watching the child rush to obey.

"I'm Ralph Chaney," the innkeeper said. "Excuse my leg. I decided not to wear it today. They're uncomfortable, you know."

Barnett wasn't sure how to react to that remark. He decided to ignore it. "You got a cabin?"

"Fifteen dollars per day. We take Visa, American Express and green money." He stared at Jay, gulping down the rest of his drink.

"We'll take it."

"You don't know how happy that makes me." Smirking, he started toward the door, then stopped. "Aren't you Barnett, of *the* Barnetts?"

"How did you know?" Jay asked, caught off-guard.

"Your picture was in the Seattle paper the other day. You wrote some book? Made a movie?"

"You certainly have an uncanny memory for faces."

"Besides," Chaney began as he limped through the screen door, "my wife talks about you all the time."

Curiosity aroused and ego flattered, Jay followed Chaney inside. "Who's your wife? Do I know her?"

"She's sure as hell goin' to be hurt if you don't," the host slurred, beckoning Barnett into the combination office-kitchen to sign the registration card. "Her grandfather built this place."

"Carol Franklin!?!"

The idea of a reunion with his first lay aroused a mixture of conflicting emotions within Jay. On the one hand, he looked forward to seeing the woman she had become and talking over old times. On the other, he still suffered mild guilt at the way he'd ended the relationship.

"Her name is Chaney, now," retorted his host, pouring himself another drink. "Isn't she lucky to have lassoed me as a husband?"

"I'd like to say 'hello.'"

"She's painting one of the cabins. I'd be doing it myself, but, then I have a good excuse." With a flourish, Chaney pointed to his empty pant leg. He handed Jay a key. "Cabin two. That's where you'll be staying and that's about where you'll find her. Have fun."

"Hey, Chaney," began Barnett gently, "I'm sorry about your accident...."

"Viet-Nam."

"Whatever, I'm truly sorry. But, it wasn't my fault. Okay?"

Chaney didn't reply. He raised his glass in a mock toast.

"Come on, Dave," Jay called. "Let's go take a look at our cabin."

The boy, halfway up an oak tree, climbed down and ran across the driveway.

"Can I carry my suitcase, Dad?"

"Why not." Jay opened the trunk of the Skylark and pulled out the luggage.

Glancing up ahead, he saw Carol on a ladder between the first two cabins, painting the roof trim. Her blue denim pants and red cotton blouse were paint splattered. Even her long auburn hair had green in it, yet those innocent banjo eyes and her full breasts had all their old appeal.

He could tell by her quizzical expression that she didn't recognize him. "Hello, Spunky," he said. "How you doing?"

"Jay!" she squealed with delight, jumping off the ladder and running over to him. She gave him a big hug and kiss. Barnett was surprised, but she'd always been short on

inhibitions. Like that unforgettable night on the beach. She
was the one who'd suggested that they go skinny-dipping.

They faced each other, assessing the changes the
years had made. She was a very attractive woman. The
button nose and freckles he'd teased her about so long ago
now made her look cuter than ever.

"What are you doing here?" she asked. I've been
reading so much about you. You're doing so well."

"I've been lucky," he replied, choosing not to dispel
her illusions. "I'm here for a little business and relaxation."

"Dad...?" Dave had been watching the reunion and
appeared baffled.

"Excuse me, Carol." Jay took his child by the hand.
"This is my son, David."

"My, but you're a big boy," she said. "I've got a son,
too, a little older than you."

"Where is he?" Dave asked.

"Oh, he's in Yakima, visiting his grandparents for a
couple of weeks. His name is Randy."

"I'd like to have met him." Jay leaned against the
picket fence that separated the Franklin Court from Fourth
Street. "How long have you been running this place? I had
visions of you living on a farm with a dozen kids."

"Not hardly," she giggled. "We took over after
Gramps died. Ralph, my husband, was injured in the war.
The family felt this would be a good, undemanding situation
for him to get into. With his military pension and all, we
make out just fine."

She noticed Dave trying to climb onto the fence.
"Careful there, honey. You might hurt yourself."

"You mind Mrs. Chaney," Jay said. "She owns this
place and if we want to stay, we have to do what she says."

"Hey, Barnett!" Ralph Chaney's shout could be heard
throughout the trailer court.

Jay saw Carol wince. "Your modern paging system?" he joked, walking around the cabin.

Chaney was on the porch, leaning on his crutches. "I hate to break up your little get-together, but you got a phone call. Take it in the kitchen." He hobbled back into the house.

Who the hell could be calling him here, Jay wondered. He strode over to the office. "This is Jay Barnett," he said into the receiver.

"Mr. Barnett, I'm Larry Palmer of the *Grant County Ledger*." The caller had a high falsetto voice that Jay didn't believe. Perhaps this was somebody he once knew playing a gag?

"What can I do for you, Mr. Palmer?"

"I heard you were in town and was hoping you might consent to an interview. 'Local boy makes good,' or something like that."

"You guys sure work fast here," Jay chuckled. "I haven't even been here an hour yet."

"Are you in Mineral lake for business or pleasure?"

"Both. There's a real estate deal, and I'm also going to relax for a few days. Maybe look up an old friend or two."

"Which friends?" The caller's voice seemed to tense.

"I don't know. Sam Jackson, probably...."

"Anybody else?"

Through the archway leading to the living room, Jay could see Chaney, sitting in an armchair, staring at him. "I'll be off in a minute," he called, covering the mouthpiece with his hand.

"Take your time," Chaney muttered, sipping from his glass. "It's the other fellow's dime."

"Mr. Palmer," Jay said to the caller, "you caught me at a bad time. Why don't you call me tomorrow after I've settled in. I'll be happy to meet with you for coffee or a drink.

"That's fine. I'll phone about noon."

"By the way," Jay said, "you've aroused my curiosity. How did you know I was at the Franklin Trailer Court?"

"I was just in the bank and they told me."

"I see...."

"Talk to you later," the man said, hanging up.

This reporter bothered him. Maybe it was his odd voice, his overly glib manner, the pointed questions, or, perhaps, the more general ones he should have asked. And, wasn't it odd that the banker knew he was at the Franklin Court when he himself hadn't even considered the place until he drove into it on an impulse fifteen minutes ago?

THREE

"I'm sorry Ralph couldn't make it tonight," Jay lied. He headed the Skylark into Mineral Lake's business district. The afternoon had been a scorcher, and now, in the cooler evening, people were on the street, though not half as many as he'd remembered from years past.

"He hasn't been feeling too well the last few days," Carol replied. "Probably some virus."

"Probably." Barnett knew the nature of Chaney's "illness". Married to a man of such a liquid disposition, Carol must have her troubles.

"Hungry, Dave?" he asked over his shoulder.

"Can I have a cheese sandwich?"

"A hamburger would be better for you."

"I want a cheese sandwich."

"You know, if you eat many more cheese sandwiches, you're going to turn into a cheese."

"Aw, Dad," Dave giggled, "I will not."

"My Randy is a hot dog freak," Carol offered, plucking a loose thread from her yellow print dress.

"Better watch out," Jay said, "he might turn into one."

The Mineral Lake Grill, with its blue stucco exterior and bubbling champagne glass sign flashing on-and-off, appeared to be doing a fair business as Barnett parked in front. Two noisy customers were leaving; five more entering. Jay wondered if there would be a long wait for a table. In L.A., restaurants took reservations. "As I recall," he said, "the food here is not too bad."

"It's better than Al's, and they have a nice bar," said Carol.

"I heard about Jerry Roscoe today. Had you seen him much in recent years?"

"Not really. You know, he was killed about seven years ago. We've only lived here just over four. I saw him back in about 1961. That was the last summer I was here. He didn't come around to the court to visit. I just bumped into him on the street. He acted sort of strange. I think he'd been drinking."

"You have no idea how he got killed? The details?"

"All I know is what I heard from neighbors. He got drunk one night and drove off a cliff. I tried to look up his parents when we moved here permanently, but his father had died and his mom had moved back where she came from. Wyoming, I think."

"I don't know," Jay pondered. "To me, it doesn't sound like the Jerry we knew. I didn't think he was the type to become a drunk."

"I heard he was on narcotics, too."

"I heard that, and that doesn't sound like Jerry either. Who knows? People change, I guess." Jay opened the door for Carol. "Come on, tiger," he said to his son, who scampered out of the back seat.

Only a few diners were in the dimly lit cafe. A blond hostess with crooked teeth sat Jay's party at once in a booth near the back where he could see the swinging doors leading to the bar. He hoped the nearby jukebox wasn't going to be fed while they were at dinner.

"This place really hasn't changed much," he said to Carol after he'd given the waitress their cocktail order and told her to bring David a grilled cheese sandwich before he fell asleep. "I think it used to be blue and orange, but, otherwise, it's the same as it was sixteen years ago. Is it still the watering hole for the town's 'founding fathers'?"

"There's no place else to go at night since they closed the movie house," she replied. "Two or three evenings a week you'll find the bigwigs boozing it up in the bar." She took a pack of cigarettes from her purse and let Jay give her a light.

"Maybe I should stick my head in there later, see if there's anyone I know," he said.

Although his firsthand recollections of Maggie Murphy were obscure, Jay recognized the immense old woman immediately when she tottered out of another booth, supported by a cane and a skinny effeminate man, dressed in suit and tie. Jay guessed him to be in his mid-forties. Maggie must weigh close to three hundred pounds, he thought. The rolls of her flesh seemed about to burst through the cotton tent she was wearing.

"Damn service is getting worse and worse here," she grumbled. Her companion pulled at his thin mustache. Barnett assumed he must be Sean, her son.

Had he been seven or eight that time she'd accosted his dad in the drug store? He and Harry had been sitting at the soda fountain, enjoying a Coke, when the irate woman had come up and screamed at his father. What had it all been about, Jay wondered.

On her way out, Maggie looked down at Jay's booth. "Good evening, Mrs. Chaney."

"Hello," Carol replied, coolly, forcing a smile at the woman's scowling moonface.

"And where is Mr. Chaney tonight?"

"Home."

"Your friend is a stranger here?" Maggie was staring hard at Jay, as though trying to recollect if she knew him.

"Mr. Barnett and his son are staying in one of our cabins," Carol responded.

"Barnett?"

"I'm Harry Barnett's son," Jay said.

"Well!" Maggie huffed. "I'd thought you Barnetts had finished with our town."

"Not quite."

"May I ask what your business is here?"

Jay had to smile at the old woman's impertinence. Before he could think of a clever answer, Carol chimed in, "He's planning to run for mayor!"

Carol's sharp retort and Maggie's face turning the color of strawberries caused Jay to burst out laughing. Carol joined him as they watched the one-time mayor move angrily out the door, her huge buttocks revolving. Sean threw an indignant look back over his shoulder, then gave his full attention to his mother.

"I can't stand her," Carol said. "My grandfather used to be pleasant to her, so ever since I've been here, she's figured she can come by and tell me how to run my life. We rented trailer space to a nice black couple two years ago, and she went right through the roof. Said nobody would come to Mineral Lake again if they heard niggers were welcome."

"She still thinks she's head honcho," Jay said. "Forget it, Spunky."

"Just last week," Carol persisted, " I was at the market and she came by with her sissy son. Told me I was buying the wrong kind of detergent. Her brand was better. Then she had the gall to take my choice out of my basket and try to replace it with hers."

Jay suddenly became aware of a middle-aged man staring at him, as if he, too, were trying to place his face. After a moment, he turned away to say something to his female dining companion. Maybe, Jay thought, the guy had seen his picture in the Seattle paper.

"So, tell me about Hollywood," Carol said. "What's it like?"

"It's very challenging, very plastic, very depressing." That was his standard response to this often asked question. "But, I love being where the action is. Just being a small part of such an exciting industry makes all the crap bearable."

"What's the name of your movie?"

"Repercussions"

"Who's in it?"

"Nobody you've ever heard of. It's aimed at the art house market. I made it to showcase my talents as a writer-director."

Carol seemed slightly disappointed. "Do you know any movie stars?" she asked.

"A few."

"What's Robert Redford like?"

"Excuse me," he laughed. "But I can't get over how 'civilians,' people like yourself, outside the movie business, always believe that everybody in Hollywood is buddies with everybody else. Do you know everybody in Mineral Lake?"

She chuckled, embarrassed. "No, but you read about all those parties and premieres...."

"Just because I go to a movie theater and Paul Newman is there doesn't mean I know him. Like every place else in the world, people in Hollywood have their own circle of friends and business associates. I'd love it, but Paul and Joanne don't have me over for dinner twice a week."

Barnett continued to expound on the Hollywood scene and his experiences with stars and frustrated would-be stars through three rounds of drinks and most of dinner. Ordinarily he would have switched the topic, but Carol's receptiveness was refreshing. Unlike his gossip-minded relatives in Seattle, she seemed truly interested in what he had to say. Her hazel eyes seldom left his.

David didn't appear to mind the monologue either. He'd fallen asleep shortly after he'd gulped down his dinner, and now presented a peaceful portrait of "Small Boy Napping."

Near the end of the meal, Jay's ramblings became more personal. Unconsciously shredding his paper cocktail napkin, he told her how he'd decided, halfway through his junior term at Northwestern University, that he didn't want to return to Seattle and take over the family jewelry business; how he'd followed his dream to Hollywood and a hoped-for career as a film producer. His folks had been upset. They were even more furious when he'd eloped with his college sweetheart, Helen, a gentile.

"What happened to your marriage?" Carol sipped her coffee slowly.

"I guess we outgrew each other. Once it became obvious that the studios weren't running after me, I got into the publicity game. Helen either wouldn't or couldn't accept what goes with that kind of life..."

He reflected a moment, then added: "She started to drink... I was having too much fun to notice... and, when I finally did, it was too late. We were beyond saving."

"That's sad," said Carol.

"I kind of feel sorry for Helen... She was a Catholic, so my family never really accepted her. She must have always felt like an outsider."

Carol studied his pensive expression for a full minute before she broke the silence. "Well, what *does* go on in the life of a publicist?"

"Long hours," he began, breaking from his momentary musing. "Attending movie premieres... parties.... Escorting female clients...."

"*That* sounds like it might have been fun for you."

"Believe it or not, it was all strictly business."

Carol didn't say a word, but flashed him a look she might have given a child who had just told her that it was a big black bear who'd eaten all the cookies in the cookie jar.

Jay took her hand in his, looked her square in the eye with mock sincerity and proclaimed, "Seriously."

They both started to laugh. She squeezed his hand with affection. Gazing at her smiling face, he felt the old spark, the same desire he'd felt on the beach sixteen years before. He wanted to hold her close, to make love to her, to apologize for the insensitive way he'd ended the relationship, to explain why he hadn't answered her letters.

There might have been a tinge of guilt in her expression, yet Jay didn't doubt that she wanted, or needed him, too.

"Aren't you the Barnett kid?"

The sharp interruption annoyed Jay. He looked up at the figure standing next to the booth. In spite of added years that had whitened thinning hair and a perennial two-day-old beard, Sam Jackson had changed little since the days of Jay's weekly visits to watch the *Mineral Lake Bulletin* being printed. Sam's face seemed gaunt, his cotton sport jacket too large, as if the publisher had recently been ill. Otherwise, with the unusual cold stogie clenched in his mouth, the editor looked like his old self.

"Hello, Mr. Jackson," Barnett grinned, rising to shake hands. "I was going to look you up tomorrow."

"I heard you were in town," Sam said, inspecting the grown-up version of the boy he'd once known. "You here on business?"

"I'm selling some land to a man from Spokane, who's decided to hang me up here until Monday. How have you been? I've thought about you often over the years."

"Okay for a young geezer of sixty-seven. I'm getting enough print orders to scratch out a living."

"Sit down." Jay indicated the space next to Carol. "Join us for an after dinner drink. Do you know Mrs. Chaney?"

"I've known Mr. Jackson since I was a teenager," interjected Carol. "He and my grandfather played Pinochle together."

"How's that husband of yours getting along?" Sam asked, sliding into the booth and motioning to the waitress.

"He's fine."

"I'd introduce you to my son," Jay said. He brushed some strands of hair out of the sleeping child's face. "But, I don't think he'd appreciate it."

"He looks a lot like you," Jackson commented, then for Carol's benefit, "You know, this guy with the beard here would hang around my office every time we printed the paper. For a while, we even let him put some copies together. You couldn't miss a Jay Barnett paper. The center fold was always crooked."

Jay chuckled and gave the waitress their drink order. "Did you sell the paper, Sam?" he asked, thinking it was out-of-character for Jackson to have ordered a double bourbon. He recalled his dad mentioning once that the editor never drank anything hard, only beer.

"Yep. After Arlene, my wife, died five years ago, the paper wasn't fun anymore. Advertising revenues were down. The *Grant County Ledger* made me a good offer. These days, when I'm not printing up handbills or business cards, I'm working on a book about my years with the *San Francisco Chronicle*, and the Mineral Lake murder."

"What murder is that?" Barnett queried.

Jackson seemed insulted. "You mean you never heard of the terrible murder we had here over fifteen years ago?"

"I was away at school then?"

"Christ, it made the wire services," scolded Sam. "I reported the thing exclusive to the entire country."

"I'm sorry." Barnett tried to avoid smirking. "Back then, I wasn't into reading the paper every day. What happened?"

"Only the most sensational murder ever committed in this part of the country."

The waitress returned with the drinks. Before she left, Jackson asked her to bring him another double.

"They found the body of a vagrant floating in the lake with his throat cut," Carol offered.

"The throat was ripped out!" insisted Sam, downing the bourbon.

"Okay, it was ripped out. There was talk of it being a kind of occult slaying, but they never found the killer."

De´ja Vu. Something about the case sounded familiar to Jay. Maybe his parents had mentioned it to him, or perhaps he was being reminded of an old movie or television show. "Were there any suspects?"

"The damn state police were in here like a bunch of Keystone Kops," Sam said. "Didn't find out a damn thing." He tried to light the remnants of his cigar, then tossed it into the ashtray and took another from his coat pocket. "It was sure the coup de grace as far as this town was concerned."

"I wanted to ask you about that," said Jay. "What's happened to all the tourists who used to come here?"

"A couple of things. First of all, people got scared off by the murder. I reported the story just the way it went down, but the Seattle and Spokane papers really sensationalized it. Said there was a mad killer running around town. A 'Jack the Ripper.' Now, who the hell would want to spend their vacation in a place where there's a gruesome unsolved murder?"

"But that was years ago...."

"Then, about the same time, your dad, fine man that he was, shut down the west beach, so there was no decent place for the tourists to swim. I know he did it to get the town out of the clutches of fat ol' Maggie, but without recreation facilities here for a couple of years, people found other places to go. By the time the town acquired the beach, it was too late. Folks had gotten out of the Mineral Lake habit."

"You know, I don't like to tell you this," Carol said candidly. "But a lot of residents around here began hating the

Barnetts. They blamed your father for destroying the town's economy."

"I *did* notice some coolness in a couple of quarters," mused Jay, looking over at the middle-aged man who had been glowering at him.

"Now, that fellow over there ran a gift shop." Sam gave the man a friendly wave. "It went bust finally. To him, 'Barnett' is a four-letter word. Don't expect the red carpet treatment."

"You don't blame my father?"

"Hell, no!" replied the newsman. "If the people of Mineral Lake, and I include myself in this category, had had the guts to oppose Maggie in the first place, all this wouldn't've happened. Harry thought that Mineral Lake could become the top health resort in this part of the country. He even bought that huge piece of real estate you folks owned with the idea of building a luxury hotel on the east half some day.

"If we'd backed him against Maggie and made conditions right for some of his rich contacts to invest outside money, we'd be the Palm Springs of the Pacific Northwest now. Instead, we're stagnating. All we get here these days are the retirees with arthritis and a smattering of regular tourists.

"Sorry if I made you nervous," he said, looking at the pile of paper shredded before Jay.

Barnett grinned sheepishly. "Some people doodle. I rip up cocktail napkins. Sometimes I even break up Styrofoam coffee cups into itsy-bitsy pieces."

"Who are you selling your acreage to?" Sam looked around for the waitress.

"His name's Gousha. I don't know too much about him, except that he wants to build a second home here. Evidently, he's got the money to afford it."

Jay and Carol both opted for coffee when the waitress returned. Jackson ordered another double. He went on bringing Jay up to date on the town's social history, rattling off local names, most of which Barnett didn't know. Others he recalled as people he'd heard his parents talk about.

"You must remember Charley Nathan?"

"Wasn't he on the city council? A fat guy?"

"We referred to him as 'portly.' He succeeded Maggie as mayor. Served for five years and, considering he was sort of intimidated by the old bitch, wasn't too bad at the job.

"Nice guy. He dropped dead of a heart attack one year into his second term."

"How about Jerry Roscoe, the fellow who was killed in an auto wreck a few years back?" Jay figured if anyone knew the inside story on Jerry, it would be Sam.

The old editor took a puff on his cigar while he pondered that one. "A tragic case," he said finally. "I didn't know the family very well, but from what I understand, they were good parents. All of a sudden, the boy, when he was in his late teens, becomes the town drunk. He was on drugs, too, they say, and he wouldn't talk to anybody. The judge over in Ephrata got tired of scolding him on drunk driving charges and sent him to the reformatory for six months."

"How did the accident happen?"

"Who knows? The kid got smashed, went joy riding and, before you know it, ran himself off a cliff. Thank God he didn't hurt anybody except himself. How well did you know him?"

"Jerry, Carol and I ran around together."

"Damn shame."

"Was it an accident, Sam," Jay asked, "or suicide?"

"They eventually listed it as an accident."

"What do you mean 'eventually'? Didn't they know?"

Jackson downed the rest of his glass. "The medical examiner, at one point, wasn't sure whether the kid could've driven the car at all with the amount of barbiturates they found in his body. He was loaded up with drugs when they did the autopsy."

Carol, who had been paying only polite attention to Sam up to this point, now gave him her full concentration. "You mean, they suspected murder?" she asked.

The old man waved his cigar. "They checked with some experts and decided that the drug level was marginal. Without any corroborative evidence to back up a suspicion of foul play, that theory was dropped."

"Dad," David mumbled, awakening with a whimper, "let's go!"

"How you doin', sleepy head?" Jay asked. "You want something more to eat?"

"No, I want to go!"

"We call him 'Mr. Charm,'" Jay quipped, dropping a few bills onto the table to cover the check. "We'd better get home, Sam. Are you going to be around the shop tomorrow, or on the weekend? I'd like to introduce you to little 'Rip Van Winkle' here when he's more up to it."

"Busy or not, I'm there six days a week." Jackson stood up. "Stop by. I've got two entire scrapbooks full of stories about our unsolved murder, if you're interested in knowing what happened."

"I'd like to look at them," Jay said. He tried to recall why the case sounded familiar. "Murder mysteries are always intriguing."

With David, still half-asleep, cradled in Jay's arms, they walked through the nearly empty dining room. At the bar's entrance, Jackson paused. "I'll say goodnight here," he said. "There's a fellow in there I want to see."

Barnett knew nobody was in the bar, but if Sam wanted to spend the night downing double bourbons, that was his affair. Apparently, being a widower and without a newspaper to keep him busy, booze was the best prescription for fighting Mineral Lake boredom and memories.

"One last question before you go, Sam," Jay said. "Do you know a reporter with the *Grant County Ledger* named Palmer? Larry Palmer?"

"No such animal," Jackson replied immediately. "I know everybody on that rag and, unless he just started this week, he doesn't exist. Somebody been pulling your leg?"

"Maybe so," Jay nodded. "Could you check and see if a Larry Palmer did start with the *Ledger* this week?"

"First thing in the morning. Call me about noon and I'll let you know."

As Carol held the outside door open for Barnett and his sleeping son, the newsman walked into the bar, showing no evidence of the six shots of eighty-proof he'd consumed during the past forty-five minutes.

"He sure fits the stereotype of the hard-drinking newspaperman," said Jay.

"He holds it well," replied Carol.

"That's part of the stereotype."

Jay felt loose, in a playful mood. He'd enjoyed a decent enough meal, some warm conversation and the old spark for Carol was building into a small flame. His smile deserted him when he saw the black letters splashed on the yellow Skylark.

"JEW BASTARD GO HOME!"

The words dripped from the hood and, for a moment, Jay was a boy again, reliving the taunts of Mineral Lake's children.

Anger overwhelmed him. Carrying his son, he stalked into the middle of the street and shouted "Fuck you, Mineral Lake! Fuck you!"

Nobody responded. Except for a few empty cars, Main Street was deserted.

FOUR

"The sheriff will be right over," said Carol, emerging from the Grill followed by Sam.

Jay didn't look up. He dunked the sponge again into the bucket of warm soapy water the restaurant had given him and scrubbed at the yellow hood. "It's coming off. Slowly, but surely."

Sam saw the words his friend was washing away, then threw his cold cigar down with disgust. "God damn it! What's the matter with this town? Hitler lives!"

"Any ideas, Sam?" Jay asked. "Who could have done it?"

"I could name you fifty people right now. All friends of Maggie."

"We had some words with her this evening." Carol offered.

"Forget her," Jay said. "She's too old and her son's not the type." He moved around to the side of the car and glanced through the window. After being jolted awake by his father's yelling, David had finally fallen asleep again in the back seat.

"It might even be somebody you've never met," said Sam. "A friend of a friend of a merchant who went out of business, some kids looking for trouble...."

"I'm not sure," replied Barnett. "Casual acquaintances don't write this kind of crap. Whoever did it is convinced my family screwed him, and he's too cowardly to say anything to my face."

Jay felt rather proud of himself. Except for the first few seconds after he'd seen the dripping paint, he'd maintained his cool throughout this incident; used his brain to analyze the situation. He could thank Carol for that.

She'd seen him starting to blow and had taken his arm. The poster paint would wash off, and the people who did it were "garbage" and didn't count. Something about the caring way she'd expressed those obvious thoughts had calmed him. If his ranting and raving was going to cause her embarrassment, then, by God, he could be a *mensch*.

"Somebody call for help?" asked the driver of the blue-and-white sheriff's car that had pulled up behind the Skylark. He was in his early thirties; dressed in a beige uniform, and wore an undersized ranger's hat atop his head, which reminded Jay of Smokey the Bear.

"Come over here, Gene, and look at this," said Sam.

The deputy made no move to get out of his car. "What's the trouble, Mr. Jackson?"

The lawman's indifference irked Jay. "The trouble is that somebody painted insults on my car," he said, walking over to glower at the deputy's acne-scarred face. "What are you going to do about it?"

The deputy gazed at him for a moment, then looked at Sam.

"Why don't you come look at the damage?" suggested Jackson.

Without comment, the officer put his car into "Park," opened the door and stepped out. He was a lanky six-foot-six and, had Jay been in a more jovial mood, he might have inquired as to how the weather was up there.

"Looks like there ain't no permanent damage," the deputy said to Sam. "What'd it say?"

"It was anti-Semitic trash," replied Jackson.

"What'd it say?"

"It said 'Jew Bastard, Go Home!'"

The officer looked over in Jay's direction, but avoided direct eye contact. "You a Jew?"

"So what?"

"Gene," Sam interjected, "I don't mean to tell you how to do your job, but Mr. Barnett's religion has nothing to do with it. The very least you've got here is a case of malicious mischief. I think you should take down a report."

"Anybody see who did it?"

"No."

"Takin' down a report would be a damn waste of time, then. It's a lot of paper work that is just goin' to get filed away and forgot about."

Jay could feel his temper boiling again, but he deferred to Sam. "Look, Gene," the editor said, moving closer, "I can phone Ed LaGrange at home right now and he'll chew your ass out. Ed and Mr. Barnett's father were very good friends."

"You want the report? You'll have the report," Gene said. "I'll get my clipboard."

"What's Ed LaGrange got to do with this?" Jay recalled how his dad had tried to help out the struggling jeweler by giving him some of his own precious stones on consignment.

"He's the sheriff now," Sam answered. "His business folded about the time Oscar Heath retired, so, since he'd been our Sunday deputy, the city council offered him Oscar's job. He and I were the ones who went out onto the lake fifteen years ago and recovered that body."

"And who's this character?" Jay asked, pointing to the deputy who was writing on his clipboard. He wondered if perhaps he had met this schmuck as a boy.

"Gene Thomas. Local farm boy. He fills in for Ed evenings and Sundays. Maybe you've met him. He's lived here since he was in his teens."

Sam turned his attention to the deputy, "Hey, Gene. You ever meet Mr. Barnett here when you were a kid? Jay, this is Gene Thomas."

Jay studied the man's face, but found nothing recognizable about it. "Hi!"

"Gene's daddy was a war hero," Jackson added.

Thomas nodded glumly, not offering to shake hands with the visitor. "The Barnetts moved away before my parents moved here." He handed Jay the clipboard and pen. "Fill out your name and address," he instructed, "then sign it." He glanced inside the Skylark at the sleeping child, then retrieved the signed document. "We'll keep you informed," he said.

Jay watched the sheriff's car disappear up Main Street. "He sure has a great personality."

"What do you expect for twelve dollars a shift?" asked Jackson. "'Adam-12'?"

It was midnight when the Skylark pulled back into the trailer court. There had been little conversation during the ride. Jay had been mulling Jackson's parting words. "Don't worry," he'd said. "Whoever did this has had his fun. He won't bother you again."

Jay hoped Sam knew what he was talking about.

Except for a streetlight illuminating the lawn area, the court was in darkness as the automobile stopped in front of cabin two. "It's been quite a night," Jay said, turning off the motor.

"Why don't you put David to bed, then meet me in cabin five," Carol suggested. Her smile left nothing to the imagination. "It's empty."

The lady's boldness surprised and also pleased Jay. But then, hadn't she'd been tentatively flirting with him all evening? "About ten minutes?" he asked.

"Ralph is usually asleep before eleven. Just let me make certain." She didn't wait for his reply, but got out of the car and hurried across the gravel.

Stripping a sleeping David down to his undershorts was always a struggle for Jay and, tonight, with the lad tossing around on his cot-sized bed, was no different. He'd just removed the child's trousers when he heard Chaney's loud voice coming from the house. The words were indistinguishable, but there was no mistaking their angry tone. Then, Carol's irate voice was giving it right back to him.

The sound of shattering glass. Jay considered walking across the court to see if she was okay. This thought sustained itself until he recalled that Chaney, despite his amputation, possessed the build of a football player. Perhaps it would be better, he reasoned, if he let Carol handle her own domestic squabbles.

More shouting. A screen door slammed open. Jay stepped outside his cabin. Lights in other cabins and trailers switched on.

Chaney, obviously drunk, was on the porch, maneuvering his crutches in an effort to maintain his balance. "I'm goin' over there an' tell him," he shouted at Carol, who was silhouetted in the doorway. "He's goin' to stay away from you, or I'll blow his fuckin' head off.!"

He started to move forward, but his crutch missed and he tumbled down the three steps onto the gravel. Hesitantly, Jay started over.

At her husband's side, Carol called, "Please go back, Jay. I'll take care of him."

She helped Chaney get up onto his crutches and assisted him back into the house. Jay knew she would be out again. He leaned against the Skylark, waiting. He'd sensed that Carol was having problems with her husband, but, Christ, he'd never figured things were this bad.

She appeared at the door a few minutes later carrying two bath towels, spotted Jay and ran over to him. "I'm sorry," she said, trying to avert her red eyes. "I didn't think he'd be up. I told him you needed extra towels...."

"How is he?"

"He's Ralph." She held back further tears. "You know, he's constantly accusing me of being unfaithful to him, but, believe it or not, tonight is the first time I'd ever even considered it. Maybe I just wanted to go back to being young again."

"How long has he been like this?"

"Since he lost his leg. He hasn't been able to adjust to it. He used to be so active. A real outdoors man. Now, he just sits and drinks. He shouts at Randy and accuses me of everything he can think of."

"Would it be easier if I moved somewhere else in the morning?"

"No. Please don't," she said. "He's taken off on you because he knows we're old friends. Every time he's read about you in the Seattle papers, he gets jealous. He feels inadequate. It's himself he's mad at, not you."

"I've got to get back," she said, handing him the towels. "I'm sorry about tonight."

Barnett took her by the shoulders. "Has he tried a shrink? They can work wonders, you know."

"He won't consider it. That's too unmanly."

"You could leave him."

"I can't," she sobbed. "He needs me and Randy. I loved him once. We had a good marriage. Really, I still hope we can put it back together again."

Jay watched her run back to the house and close the door. A moment later, the lights went out and all was quiet, except for the crickets.

He'd almost forgotten about those noisy little bastards that used to serenade him to sleep at night.

Jay lay awake on his hard bed for over an hour. The dark cabin was stuffy, and even leaving one window open gave little relief from the hot summer night. Staring through the screen door into the court, he remembered the good times with Carol. Perhaps he'd be doing her a favor to move out in the morning. After all, what could he offer her? A quick roll in the hay? And, who knew how Chaney would finally react to an actual infidelity on her part if he found out. Maybe it would be best if he just moved over to the Royal Inn.

He drifted off slowly.

Through barely open eyes, Jay became aware of movement. A shadow on the other side of the screen. The outline of a man. A large man. He gazed at it, accepting the form, which seemed to be peering in at him, as a dream.

The rattle of the hooked screen door, as the figure tried to gain entry, brought Jay fully awake. "Who is it?" he said, quickly sitting up in bed. "Who's there?"

He blinked. The figure had gone.

He was across the room in three steps, unlatched the doors, and stepped onto the sharp gravel. Nobody was in sight. Not a sound, except for the crickets. And, in the air, the faint, but unmistakable, odor of gasoline.

FIVE

"Wake up, Dad. It's morning."

His head deep in his pillow, Jay opened one eye and tried to bring his wristwatch into focus. God, the cabin was hot.

"I saw your eye open," the boy squealed with glee. "You're awake."

Seven o'clock. That's all Jay needed; to go through the day with only four hours sleep. "Daver," he mumbled. "Please let me sleep for a while longer. I didn't fall asleep 'til after three."

"But, I want to see the Storyman. You promised."

"We'll see him, but he won't be awake now. Get one of your books out of the suitcase and just let me rest some more. Daddy's very tired."

Jay tried, but once awakened, he could never fall asleep again, particularly with things on his mind.

Yesterday had been such a bummer. What had he done to deserve all this?

Who the hell was that Nazi prick who had painted those words on his car?

In all Jay's years, he had never...*never* personally experienced any direct anti-Semitism. Certainly it was all around him in Mineral Lake, but when he was younger, it just hadn't penetrated.

It had been a weird day, too. Who the hell was Larry Palmer? If he wasn't a reporter, why had he phoned him?

Then, there had been that dream, or had somebody really tried to get into his cabin last night? He wasn't sure.

"Come on, Dad," David insisted, bouncing up and down to give his bed's springs a workout. "Get up, get up, get up!"

"Okay, tiger. Just give me a minute." Jay sat up in bed and looked around. Early Salvation Army, this room. Miscellaneous beds, dresser and chair, complemented by varnished knotty pine paneling.

"Let's go see the Storyman, Dad." Dave flung himself onto Jay's bed.

"The boy's like a kitten," Jay thought. "If he wasn't so cute, he'd be dead."

"It's still early, tiger" he said. "Besides, first we're going to have breakfast, then I've got to put some gas into the car, and then I've got to stop off at the bank again to cash a check. Daddy spent most of his money for dinner last night."

"Can I play on the swings today?"

"All right. We'll see." He figured that, for five minutes, Maggie wouldn't notice if David utilized her facilities.

Jay headed for the bathroom. He stripped off his pajama bottoms and stepped into the shower. Like the rest of the cabin, the porcelain-tiled stall was a tight fit and, more than once, he collided with the shower head.

Under the meager spray, he decided on the day. They would split from Mineral Lake. Maybe he was paranoid, but the previous twenty-four hours had been too unsettling. Why should he stay in a town where most of the people hated his guts?

Damn his father's stubbornness anyway.

Blue lake was less than an hour's drive. He and David could get a cabin there, spend the weekend fishing and swimming, then be back here at the bank Monday morning with no sweat. Good idea!

By eight, Dave had agreed with the new itinerary and the pair, dressed in matching blue Levi outfits, were heading out the cabin door. Hell, Jay thought, unbuttoning his already sweat-soaked shirt, today was going to be another scorcher.

He could hear voices coming from some of the units, though none of the guests had ventured out into the trailer court this morning. Carol, however, was up and out watering the lawn, dressed in white shorts that clung snugly to her behind and a brief halter. She turned and smiled at Jay as he drove past.

"I could be arrested for what I'm thinking," he quipped, giving her scant outfit a lecherous leer.

"Come by sometime when I'm sunbathing on the roof," she said, wiggling her hips. "I wear even less."

"Everything okay?" he asked.

"It always is the morning after."

"Good." He momentarily considered telling her that they were checking out, then decided to wait until later. "See you in a couple of hours." He headed the car toward the business area.

An elderly couple, in drab bathing suits and carrying a load of beach gear, were heading down toward the lake; a well-tanned child, slightly older than David, was walking with a black cocker spaniel beside him; and a teenage boy was mowing the lawn of a frame house across the street from the old Barnett home. Automobile traffic was almost totally absent, except for a red Ford Mustang that was making a left turn at First Street. Indeed, Jay spotted only two vehicles parked on main, a beige Dodge Coronet with a smashed rear fender, and a blue Chevy van.

Al's Cafe, located in the building next to Sam Jackson's print shop, had been tagged "the grease plate" by his father. After a couple of poor meals there, the Barnett family had never eaten at Al's again.

Jay was not surprised to find the joint, with its dozen counter stools and four private booths, bustling. It was the only place in town where one could buy breakfast these days.

At David's request, they sat at the counter. Jay ordered bacon and scrambled eggs, and Dave had three slices of toast and jam and two bowls of Rice Krispies. Al's was still "the grease plate."

Leaving the cafe, Jay considered stopping next door to see Sam, but figured the editor wouldn't be in yet. He wanted to say "good-bye," and please the old man by looking at his scrapbook on the long ago murder. Damn, why couldn't he remember why the case sounded so familiar?

There would be time to visit Sam after they saw the Storyman, and before they left for Blue Lake.

Waldo's Corner Texaco Service was still at the east end of town, the last chance to fill-er-up before one took the highway north. As Jay remembered, there wasn't another gas station before Blue lake.

"Fill 'er with regular," Barnett said to the stringy dark-haired attendant with high forehead and Dumbo ears.

"What was that?" The attendant glanced up from his Spiderman comic book.

"Regular," Jay repeated, wondering if the guy's uniform had had its annual washing yet this year. "Fill it."

"Right."

Jay had recognized this wiry-framed jerk the moment he'd seen him, but he was in no mood to renew acquaintance. The prick's name was Claude. Claude Bates. And, way back when, he was one of the kids who labeled Jay with tags like "rich Jew boy" and "tourist bastard."

Sure, the son of a bitch was jealous of the Barnett family wealth. Sure, he had a sadistic, alcoholic father who used him nightly as a punching bag and even damaged the hearing in one ear. Jay could understand all that. But, the s.o.b. had helped make his younger days in Mineral Lake miserable. It might be childish, but Jay planned to go right on hating the bastard.

"Seven dollars even." Bates was back at the window with his hand extended. He seemed put out when Jay gave him a credit card.

"Goddamn illiterate," Jay said under his breath, watching him struggle to write out the sales slip.

"What'd you say, Dad?" Dave asked from the seat next to him.

"Nothing, tiger. Just mumbling to myself."

Bates looked up sharply and stared in Barnett's direction.

"Brilliant," Jay said aloud, accepting the inevitable. "You've remembered the name."

With a surly smile, the attendant sauntered back to the Skylark and handed Jay the small green tray with ticket attached. "Well, the tourist returns," he said with a superior air.

"I beg your pardon?" Barnett gave him a blank look, having decided that he would irritate this jerk most by pretending not to remember.

"Don't you remember me? I'm your old friend, Claude Bates."

"Sorry," Jay's voice was curt. "I have no friend named Claude Bates."

"Come on, Barnett. Don't play the rich stuck-up tourist with me. Maybe you don't want to remember."

"May I have my card back, please?"

"You mean, you really don't remember me?"

"To tell the truth, Claude, I do," Jay said, starting the car and putting it into gear. "And, really, I'm impressed with how far you've come up in the world."

He pressed down on the gas pedal, leaving Bates standing by the pumps, trying to decipher his parting remark. By this afternoon, Jay figured, the putz may have realized that he'd been insulted.

They were parked in front of the bank at ten o'clock sharp.

"The swings, Dad, the swings," Dave reminded as he climbed out of the car.

Barnett looked over at the play yard next to Murphy's Hotel. It was empty. Taking his son by the hand, he stepped out into the street, paused to let a blue Chevy van pass, then quickly walked across. "Now, I want you to stay right here until I come for you," he cautioned. "You're not to cross the street by yourself."

"Okay, Dad," Dave agreed.

"I'll be back in five minutes, and we'll go to see the Storyman. If anyone asks you to leave, wait here on the sidewalk for me. But, don't cross the street alone." He gave the lad a pat on the behind, then watched him go through the gate and clamber up the metal slide before he walked back across the street to the bank.

"Hello," he said to the sourpussed matron who'd greeted him the day before. "May I speak to Mr. Parish?"

Still scowling, the woman rose and trotted to the bank manager's door, knocked, stuck her head inside and returned. "He'll be with you in a moment."

Jay found her sullenness amusing. "I'm curious," he said. "What did my father do to wrong you?"

Her lips pinched tightly together and face flushed, the teller simply glowered at him.

"How are you today, Mr. Barnett?" Parish said, behind him. "Did you find a place to stay?"

"I'm over at the Franklin Court," Jay replied, realizing now for certain that Larry Palmer was unquestionably a liar. "My son and I are going up to Blue Lake for the weekend."

"I hope the fishing is good. How may I be of service?"

"Can you cash a check for me? This unexpected layover has left me a bit short."

"How large a check?"

"Two hundred dollars should do it. I've got all the proper identification."

"I think we can handle that."

Jay wrote a check. Parish copied down the numbers from his California driver's license, American Express and Visa cards, then handed the paper to a pudgy girl teller. "If I can be of further help, please let me know," the manager said, excusing himself. "Otherwise, I'll see you Monday morning."

"Will twenties be okay?" the girl asked.

"That's fine," Jay replied. "Maybe a couple of tens, too."

The teller had just finished counting out the bills when the phone next to her rang. "Mr. Barnett," she said with surprise, "it's for you."

"Every place I go, I get phone calls." Jay shook his head, wondering if it would be Larry Palmer again.

"Barnett?" The thin, raspy voice on the other end of the line sent a chill through Jay. It was straight out of the Boris Karloff films that had scared him as a child.

"Who is this?"

"We got your son," the voice continued. "If you ever want to see him alive again, you'll do what I say."

"What are you talking about?" Jay replied, an anxious titter invading his tone. "He's right across the street."

He glanced out of the bank's picture window, but the Skylark and a gray Buick parked in front blocked his view. "Hold on a minute." Jay set the receiver down. "Please don't touch that phone," he shouted at the girl. "I'll be right back."

Barreling out of the bank, Jay couldn't believe this was happening. It was like some lousy movie. He'd left David not five minutes ago out in plain sight for the world to see. How could he have been kidnapped? This was some sort of joke. But, then, where was his boy?

The play yard looked empty.

Jay raced across the street, his eyes desperately searching the slide, swings, sandbox, every corner of the fenced facility. Perhaps Dave was playing a trick on him, hiding behind the slide.

Once inside the fence, Jay knew this was a hollow hope. Nobody was in the yard except for himself. His son was gone.

He stood… dazed. Suddenly, he felt weak. "Oh, my God, David!" he cried. He grabbed at the slide to keep his knees from buckling. It was like the times his father had been coming after him with the baseball bat.

SIX

Jay was still numb as he reentered the bank, oblivious of the employees who were staring at him. His eyes were fixed on the telephone receiver he'd left lying at the teller's cage.

"Is everything all right, sir?" the pudgy girl asked, noting his paled complexion.

He looked at her blankly for a moment, then turned his back and spoke softly into the phone. "Where is he?" The words seemed to stick in his throat. "What have you done with my son?"

"You do what you're told," said the raspy voice," and you'll see your son again."

"What do you want?"

"Don't tell no one what's going on. You understand?"

"Yes."

"There's several of us in on this. We're watchin' you close. Speak to anybody...pass a note...make a phone call to the cops, and we'll know it. That's it then for your kid. He's dead! Got it?"

An image of David's face being pushed underwater flashed through Jay's mind. "Okay," he said, "what the fuck do you want?"

"Calm, now," the voice soothed mockingly. "You don't want the people in the bank to think somethin's wrong, do you? That was rule one."

"Please," Jay replied in a hoarse whisper, "tell me what you want from me."

"I'll say this just once. Hang up the phone, then very slowly...calmly...leave the bank. Drive back to the Texaco station where you were earlier. Remember?"

"I remember."

"There's a phone booth behind the building. I'll call you at that number in exactly ten minutes. Be there. I'm only going to let it ring twice."

The phone clicked. The line was dead.

Jay stared at the electronic instrument in his hand, still not sure all this was real. But, if he was having a nightmare, why couldn't he wake up?

"Mr. Barnett, are you okay?"

Jay gazed over at the banker standing next to him. His concerned voice seemed to be coming from across the room.

"Mr. Barnett!" Parish shook his shoulder gently, penetrating the trance. "Is something wrong?"

Pressing his hand against his forehead, Jay tried to bring the bizarre events of the past few minutes into focus. The whole thing was spinning around in his brain and none of it wanted to fall into place. God, how wanted to hit something.

"If you're not well," Parish persisted, "I can drive you over to the hospital."

"*Calm,*" the caller had cautioned. Nobody in the bank was to know that anything was amiss. Barnett took a deep breath and tried to compose himself. "I'm fine," he said finally. "I just had some disturbing news from Los Angeles and it gave me a headache. Everything's okay now."

"I've got some aspirin in my office."

"No, please forget it. I'm sorry if I alarmed you." A vision of the last time he'd seen David pushed its way into his mind. The boy had been struggling up the slide.

"Jesus," Jay thought, "what if this creep is a child molester?"

Now was not the time for tears. The wall clock read twenty-five after ten. Raspy voice had given him just ten minutes to get back to Waldo's. He had to get moving.

Parish and the two tellers continued to watch him through the window as he fumbled to unlock his car door. His trembling fingers dropped the keys twice before he slid behind the wheel, wiped his moist palms on his pants and started the engine.

Failing to check the traffic flow behind him, Jay threw the transmission into "reverse," and pressed down hard on the gas pedal. The Skylark shot out into the street. An eastbound vehicle screeched to a halt.

He glanced at his rearview mirror, taking little note of the beige car he'd just missed. "Fucking son-of-a-bitch," he shouted in frustration, "stay out of my way!" He straightened the Skylark and raced down the street. A siren in his wake made him quickly check the mirror again. Momentarily, he considered outrunning the flashing red light, but, then if he went to jail, how would he help David?

He pulled to the curb. The sheriff's car stopped behind him.

"God damn it!" he swore as he watched the tall officer, citation book in hand, walking toward his vehicle. He checked his watch. Ten twenty-eight. "Shit!" He didn't have time for this. David needed him. The phone at Waldo's would be ringing in less than seven minutes, and that was two blocks away.

Jay felt the rapid, intense pounding in his chest and wondered if he was going to have a heart attack. He had to slow down; talk his way out of this. He'd charmed cops before. Now, if he could only take hold of himself and....

"Out of the car," the sheriff commanded, standing back a few feet and unsnapping his holster.

Barnett could see that this guy meant business. Maybe he thought he'd captured some dope dealer or a fleeing felon. Why else would he be ready to draw his revolver?

The Hollywood publicist stepped from the Skylark and tried to flash the smile he reserved for only the most difficult of newspaper columnists. The cop's eyes did not smile back. "Officer, please forgive me," Jay said. "I wasn't thinking." He deliberately employed large gestures away from his body, lest the lawman think he was reaching for a weapon.

"You almost smashed into me, Mister," said the sheriff, opening his citation book. "We don't like people speeding down our streets."

"I'm sorry. I had something urgent on my mind."

"Maybe a hundred dollar fine and a night in jail will help you to think more clearly. Let's see your license."

Jay handed him the license. "California, huh?" the officer said, giving him another once-over.

Suddenly Jay knew that getting out of this one was going to be a "piece of cake." At least, it had better be.

"Aren't you Ed LaGrange?" he asked.

The middle-aged lawman had lost most of his blond hair, acquired a generous paunch and sagging jowls, but Barnett still recognized him as the struggling jeweler his father had helped many years before.

"That's right. Do I know you?" LaGrange took a second look at the California license.

"I'm Jay Barnett. Harry Barnett was my father."

"For Christ's sake," the cop beamed without a moment's hesitation. "Why didn't you say so?" He shut his citation book and took Jay's hand in his. "Hell, I haven't seen you since you were a kid."

"Sixteen years." Jay breathed a silent sigh of relief. He briefly considered asking for LaGrange's help, then dismissed the thought. The kidnapper could be watching and, if he was, explaining this chance meeting was going to be problem enough.

"I saw the report about the trouble you had last night," LaGrange said, "but I didn't connect your name."

Jay glanced at his watch. Four minutes, and then that phone would start ringing. "It wasn't the most pleasant experience."

"I don't care what the s.o.b.s in this town say. Your father was a good man. Your brother, Alan, could use a lesson in being neighborly, but Harry sure did right by me. My store wouldn't've kept going for half as long as it did if it wasn't for the merchandise he lent me. God rest his soul, I say."

"Thank you," Jay replied. He contemplated what LaGrange meant when he mentioned Alan. There was no time to pursue that now. "Dad was very fond of you, too."

LaGrange seemed pleased to hear that. "I'm the full time sheriff, now." he said. "Ever since ol' Oscar Heath retired."

"Congratulations," Jay said, not quite sure how he should respond.

"What are you doing in town?" LaGrange asked.

"Business," Jay answered. This was the perfect opportunity to get away from this well-meaning hick. "That's why I was in a hurry. I'm expecting an urgent call in a couple of minutes."

"Maybe you'd like to come by for supper tonight? The wife would love to have you."

"I don't think that I can...."

"You know, Harry was like a father to me. Mine died when I was two. I'd just like to sit around and talk about him. It would mean a lot."

Jay was starting to feel sorry for the guy. "Sure," he agreed, opening the car door. It was easier to acquiesce. He could always bow out later. "I'll be there."

"Where are you staying?"

"Franklin Court." He was behind the wheel, starting the motor.

"I'll pick you up at six."

"Fine."

"And, Jay...." The cop put his paw on his shoulder. Two minutes to go. Barnett strained to be polite. "Drive carefully."

"I promise." He eased the Skylark forward, increasing the speed to thirty as he proceeded down Main toward the service station.

The phone was silent when Jay bounded out of the car, heading for the booth. He was nearly a minute late. Had he missed the call?

He leaned against the dirty glass cell, staring at the phone, waiting for it to ring. The motor of the Skylark hummed behind him. A few feet away, a brown-and-white dog, a border collie/spaniel mix, was trying to maneuver the lid off of a trash can.

He checked the receiver. The familiar buzzing that changed into a dial tone at the drop of a dime was present. The gadget was working properly.

This bastard had to call, Jay reasoned. He wouldn't've gone to the trouble of kidnapping David, then abandon the plan because of a one-minute delay. Maybe he was giving Jay a few more minutes to get to the phone. Sure, that was it. The damn thing would ring any second now.

Then, perhaps the guy had seen him talking to LaGrange and panicked. Oh, God, no! He'd at least go through with this call to see what happened. Wouldn't he?

The shrill ringing of the phone startled Jay. He grabbed at the receiver, but it slipped from his sweaty palms. "Hello," he shouted.

"Thought you'd missed me?" Raspy Voice chuckled.

"I got here as fast as I could."

"What kept you?"

"I had a problem getting out of the bank. The manager thought I was sick. He wanted to call me a doctor."

"How much did you tell him?"

"It's all right. I didn't tell him a damn thing. Look, where's my son?" Jay felt that the fragile dam holding back his tears was about to crack.

"Don't shout at me," the caller said softly. "I'm in control here. All I have to do is hang up and it's all over. See...."

The phone clicked. "No, don't do that," Jay yelled into the dead instrument. "Please don't hang up."

He slammed the receiver back into its cradle. "God damn it!" he swore, kicking the booth. What the hell should he do now? There was no guarantee that the bastard was going to call back. Should he go to the sheriff, or simply wait?

"Lose yer dime, Barnett?" said Claude Bates. He had strolled over from the station and was standing next to the Skylark. Startled, the brown-and-white dog dashed away. "If you leave yer engine running like this, you'll waste a lot of gas."

Jay mulled the attendant's cocky attitude. Was Claude just doing his usual needling, or did he know what was going on?

The phone screamed again. "Yeah!" Jay yelled into the receiver. He closed the booth door and turned his back to Bates.

"Did I make my point?" Raspy Voice asked.

Barnett softened his tone. "Please, what do you want?"

"It's gonna cost you one hundred thousand bucks to get yer kid back."

"But, I don't have...." Jay started to protest.

"Let me finish!" The caller's voice became harsh. "You leave for Seattle right away. Get the money together in used tens and twenties. On Monday, noon sharp, be in the lobby of the Olympic Hotel. You'll be paged."

"I want to talk to David."

"Later. He'll be okay just as long as you follow directions."

"I'm not doing a fucking thing until I can talk to him," Jay insisted.

"You can't now. He's on his way to Seattle. But, you can talk to him before the exchange is made. Take it or leave it."

"Okay."

""I want you on yer way within twenty minutes," Raspy Voice said. "Even with all that Barnett money, it's goin' to take you some time to come up with that kind of cash."

"There's a problem." Jay figured he'd better level with the son-of-a-bitch now.

"What?"

"No way can I come up with a hundred grand." Silence from the other end of the line. "Hello? Hello," Jay said, wondering if the guy had hung up.

"Don't fuck with us," Raspy Voice said finally. "Ain't your son's life worth that much?"

"Of course it is! But, I've never had that kind of money." Jay saw Bates move into his line of vision. The attendant continued to study him.

"What about all the dough you make in Hollywood?" the caller asked.

"Everything I have is tied up in a movie, and even that's in hock."

"How about family? Friends?"

Jay sensed some insecurity in the caller's voice. "Impossible!" he said. "They don't have it either. Look, I can get you twenty-five thousand cash by Monday morning. "I'm picking up the money at the bank here at ten."

"That's not enough."

"That's all I got, Mister," Jay pleaded. "I was going to use it to buy my film back from the lab."

"It's not enough," the caller repeated.

"Maybe I can borrow a couple thousand more in Seattle, but that's it."

"I'll hang up the phone and you'll never hear from me again."

"Please," said Jay. "I'm not kidding. I'm being straight with you now, so there won't be problems later. Monday at eleven, I'll drop the money anywhere you want."

The kidnapper hesitated. Obviously, he was trying to mentally rework his plan. "Why can't you get the money today?"

"The man who's paying me won't be here 'til Monday."

"What if you went to Seattle now, tried to raise some more cash, and completed your deal through the mail?"

An odd suggestion, mused Jay. One would think that the kidnappers would want to avoid delays. "I probably wouldn't get the twenty-five thousand then until the end of the week, even if they wired it. There are papers to be signed first. Can't we do it here?"

"No! The exchange will be made in Seattle.' The caller paused for further thought. "Okay, you pick up the cash on Monday, then head right for Seattle. We'll change the contact time to five o'clock at the Olympic."

"I can make that easy," Jay agreed with a sigh of relief.

"One thing, though," the kidnapper continued. "You're going to be watched. You don't speak to no one. No phone calls. The cops get word of this and we'll know. I don't want you out of yer cabin except for meals. Twice a day, once in the morning and again at night, you can go up to Al's Cafe for twenty minutes. But, that's all. If you fuck up just once, it's all over. You'll never hear from us again."

"When can I talk to my son?"

"When I'm ready. Now, get back to your cabin and stay there."

The caller hung up. Jay knew he wouldn't ring again. There was no reason. He'd made his point.

Barnett felt anger; the anger that evolves from frustration. The bastard and his accomplices had stolen his son. What they might be doing to the boy, he didn't want to imagine. They were demanding one hell of a ransom for David, virtually every cent Jay possessed. And, even after he'd paid it, he still had no guarantees the child would be returned alive.

"Hey, Barnett," Bates tapped on the glass. "If you're finished, I want to call my girlfriend."

Jay pushed open the door and stepped out. He didn't look at Bates, who couldn't resist one last remark. "Who were you talkin' to?" he quipped. "Yer fuckin' rabbi?"

That did it!! Bates had said the wrong thing and he was elected. Like a panther, Jay leaped at him. He grabbed the startled attendant by the shirt front, threw him to the ground and pounced. His first punch sent blood spurting from Bates' nose. The second caught him hard on the cheek.

This was perhaps the third time in his life when his rage had allowed Jay to put aside his fear of violence. He hated the kidnapper. He hated this town and its people. He hated Bates, who got the blows meant for all the others.

"Where is he?' Jay shouted. "What have you done with him, you son-of-a-bitch!?!"

Bates tried to protect his face with his hands, but Jay pulled them away and clawed at his cheeks. "Get off me! I didn't do nuthin' to you!"

Barnett pressed his thumbs on the man's throat and squeezed. "Don't! I'm sorry I teased you!" Bates sobbed. "Please...."

Jay pulled his hands back. He'd almost killed this little prick. The thought terrified him. He jumped up and ran to his car.

The attendant sat up in time to see the Skylark tear out of the station, heading east. At the corner, it made a sharp left onto the road that ran along the lake shore.

"I'll get you for this, you Jew Bastard!" Bates said, wiping the blood from his nose. "I'll fix you damn good!"

SEVEN

The Skylark darted in and around the cliffs as if it were entered in the Grand Prix. The road was narrow, running the length of the lake's three-mile shoreline. It had been cut from the weather-worn walls decades ago, and was now dotted with chuck holes.

Jay didn't know why he was on this north-bound course. He'd fled the service station in a panic, with no idea of where he was going. His attack on Bates had further unnerved him, compounding his confusion.

The last time he'd lost his temper like that was about a year ago. He'd stopped by a Luckys supermarket late one night to pick up a few items, and, while standing in the check-out line, some little schmuck with a Van Dyke beard had walked up and spit on him.

He'd spit on him!

Without a second thought, Jay had grabbed the guy, picked him up and tossed him across the aisle. He landed hard on his ass, but before he could retaliate, a couple of the store's more muscular employees had taken him by both arms and hustled him out of the store.

Apparently, the bozo had been spitting on the store's customers throughout the day, and Jay had been the first person to do something about it.

Jay felt safe in his speeding car. The turn onto the lake road had been made without thinking, but, now, as he maneuvered the sharp curves, Jay's fury was slowly vanquished. He began to relax; to let his mind filter things into their proper perspective.

If he remembered correctly, there was a spot up the road where he could turn his car around. He had to get back to the trailer court before the kidnappers became suspicious. Once there, he'd take a Valium, then try to think this horror out in detail. There were certain elements that just didn't add up, and, despite his emotional pain, worrying about David's safety was not going to help right now.

Easier said than done. He was *sick* with worry.

Nevertheless, if Jay were to have any chance of saving his son, then he was damn well going to have to develop a plan.

He wondered if Bates might report to LaGrange what had happened. Well, if he did, he'd just have to lie; tell Ed that Claude had hit him first. What else could he do? Go to jail?

The turn-out was situated on the shore side, just before the road jutted inward to disappear around a bend. It was a thin strip of land, rising ten feet above the murky water and barely large enough to accommodate two autos parked end-to-end. Bracing this filled earth from tumbling into the lake was a stack of cut boulders.

Barnett swung his car onto the strip and paused, caught by the bleak lake side view of the resort over a mile away. Sprinkled with an array of indistinct structures that broke up the monotony of its vast unimproved acreage, the village reminded Jay of one of those old sepia photographs he'd seen of America's early pioneer towns.

His attention zoomed-in on the bluff which seemed to divide the town into halves, the eastern business district, such as it was, and the residential area to the west. The mound of jagged black boulders rising out of the water was still an ominous sight to Jay. As kids, he and Jerry had dubbed the thing "Dead Man's Bluff." Today, in particular, that name still made him shiver.

More sinister was the dark empty shell atop the palisade, the burned-out bath house. He well recalled the time they had bravely climbed Dead Man's Bluff to explore the weird ruin, which Jerry claimed was haunted. They saw no ghosts, but the stench from the mud pools was so bad that both boys had become nauseous.

Jay backed the Skylark onto the road and headed toward town. Even with his fears about David, he couldn't help thinking that somewhere along this stretch was where Jerry had plunged to his fiery death.

Only Chaney was about when Jay got back to the court. The innkeeper was sitting in a lawn chair, reading the previous day's edition of the *Seattle Times*. Jay was surprised to see him sipping from a coffee mug.

"How ya' doin'?" Chaney called, in what appeared to be a sincere attempt at friendliness.

Jay's response was noncommittal. "Good morning." He locked the car and headed for his cabin. He needed that Valium.

"Hey, wait a minute." Chaney pulled himself up onto his crutches and hobbled over. He was wearing his artificial leg. "I wanna talk to you."

Surprised by the man's cordiality, Barnett hesitated. He prayed his host would make it brief.

"I wanna apologize for the way I acted yesterday," Chaney said, avoiding direct eye contact. "It was wrong of me."

"We all have our bad days, Ralph. Think nothing of it." He turned toward his cabin, but the man took hold of his arm.

"It's been rough ever since I got back from 'Nam. I guess I nip from the bottle too much."

Jay felt sorry for him. Another time, he might even have done a little hand holding; played psychiatrist, so to speak. Not today, however. He had his own problems. "With a girl like Carol on your side," he said, "I know you'll be able to work things out okay."

"Thanks for understanding." Chaney seemed to resent Jay's superficial responses. His pleasantness dissipated as he watched Jay enter his cabin. "Enjoy yer stay!" he spat.

Barnett didn't like what he'd done. Carol's husband had come to him, seeking perhaps a friend, and he'd given him the brush-off. Maybe, before he left town, he could make it up to the guy, but not now.

He fished the bottle of tranquilizers out of his suitcase and, without using water, swallowed two. Like a nervous rat in a cage, he began to pace his hot, cramped quarters.

He was seeing his predicament more clearly now. Aside from any psychological traumas his son was experiencing, a subject he preferred not to consider if he was to maintain his objectivity, Jay was relatively certain that David was well, and would be until he delivered the ransom money. The kidnappers were sure to let him talk to the child on the phone. He'd insist on it.

He's also insisst that David be present when the exchange was made. Hopefully, they'd agree.

After that, he didn't know what he'd do. He wasn't John Wayne or Clint Eastwood. He couldn't take on these bastards single-handed. Yet, if he didn't take some positive action, David would be killed right after he dropped off the money. He was sure of that. The boy, after all, was the prime witness. From the kidnappers' point-of-view, murder was the only logical course to take.

He had to get help from the police or the F.B.I.. They knew how to handle these things. They could cover him when he went to the rendezvous; make sure that neither he nor David got hurt.

But, then, how was he going to contact the authorities? This was a small town and the bastards had hinted that they had a connection with the local police, or the phone company. If he tried to get help now, they might find out, then, one day, David's body would be found by a roadside.

Stop! He couldn't think about that.

No, there'd be time in Seattle to slip away into a crowd; to make that call. On the other hand, surely his adversaries had planned for that possibility. Perhaps they weren't going to let him get to a phone in Seattle.

Perhaps they would ambush him outside of the city, unless, of course, he didn't exchange the cashier's check until he got to a Seattle bank. That wasn't a bad idea.

Perhaps, perhaps, perhaps. The possibilities were endless.

The pills began to have their effect. He discarded his sweaty shirt, propped some pillows against the wall and sat back onto his bed.

Who the hell could have pulled this thing off so quickly? He'd been in Mineral lake for less than twenty-four hours, yet this plan, ostensibly involving several people, had been formulated and put into action in that short a period.

How could David have been snatched off the street almost before his eyes?

He wasn't sure where to start looking for the answers. He started to drift off.

"Hello, hello, hello." Carol was at the screen door, still in her skimpy outfit. "Aren't you roasting in there?"

"A little bit." He was glad to see her friendly face. "Come in."

She sat across from him on the other bed. "Ralph tells me he apologized."

"Yeah, I'm afraid I wasn't very gracious. I had something on my mind, and I was short with him."

"Where's David?"

The question caught him off-guard. He reached for an answer. "I...I left him with a friend for a while."

"Who's that?"

"Mr. O'Neil. You remember Albert O'Neil, the Storyman?"

"Are you sure that's a good idea?" She appeared troubled. "Don't you know about him?"

"Know what?"

"Last year, there was an accusation, an incident with a little boy. The sheriff looked into it, but...."

"Child molestation?"

"That's what the parents said, though O'Neil was never actually charged."

"Come on, Carol. I don't believe that. I followed him around for years. So did you. He's a harmless old man."

"All I know is this kid went swimming out at his place, in that mud hole he calls a pool, and, the next day, the boy's parents reported him."

"What *exactly* was he supposed to have done?"

He knew she was on the spot now, and a little embarrassed being there. "I don't know," she said. "What do those kind of people do to children?"

"If no charges were brought against him, there couldn't have been much of a case."

"I don't think the parents wanted to put their child through the emotional hardship of a trial. But, ever since then, every parent in Mineral Lake has kept their kids away from the old man."

Jay recalled the previous day's meeting with O'Neil. "No wonder he was so happy to meet David," he said, thinking that, by all rights, father and son should be out at the Storyman's place right now, listening to his tales.

"Really, Jay," Carol persisted, "I wouldn't leave Dave alone with him. Why take chances?"

"Forget it," he replied. Under the circumstances, Carol's fears were academic. Or, were they?

She'd given him an idea. A far-fetched one to be sure, but, at this juncture, Jay was willing to tackle any long shot if it would help him to get David back. Now, he needed her knowledge of Mineral Lake. He swung around and put his feet onto the floor. "Carol, can I trust you?"

"With anything but money," she smiled.

"I need your help. But, I want you to swear that what I tell you won't leave this room."

"Call me 'Father Carol,'" she giggled. "What's the problem?"

Should he tell her or not, he pondered. One wrong word from her, and....

Still, he had to confide in someone.

"David's gone," he said finally. "He's been kidnapped."

"What!?!" She looked like possibly she hadn't heard him. "Be serious."

"I'm not joking. I left him in the play yard by Murphy's Hotel while I was in the bank. I could see the yard through the window." This retelling wasn't easy. As the words came, his eyes filled with tears. "I only looked away for a minute. And, he was gone. Jesus, if I'd just taken him into the bank with me, he'd be here right now."

He was sobbing uncontrollably. She shifted over to his bed and held him to her breast.

"I'm sorry," he said after a moment, "but this whole thing is so eerie. I feel like I'm a character in a movie." He wiped his eyes, then blew his nose into a handkerchief. "I only wish I'd read the script."

"How do you know he's been kidnapped?" she asked. "Couldn't he have wandered away?"

As she listened incredulously, Jay told her about the mysterious phone call and the subsequent race to the Texaco station to garner further instructions. He left nothing out; the fight with Bates, his drive along the lake, and the theories and plan of action he'd been formulating since returning to the cabin.

"I think you're all wrong, Jay," she announced after he'd finished. "Call in the authorities now. Otherwise, you're playing into the kidnappers' hands. They're trying to keep you isolated from getting any help."

"I can't do anything while I'm in Mineral Lake," he insisted. "Maybe the guy's bull-shitting me, but he says he'd know if I did something like that. I'm not going to take the chance."

What if *I* called?"

"No!" He was adamant. "I don't want to chance it. They may have a way of overhearing phone calls. There's electronic zoom microphones that can pick up conversations over a block away. How can we be sure they don't have something like that?"

"What do you want to do, then?"

"I don't know yet, but my gut tells me that David is still in Mineral Lake."

"But, the man said...."

"He was too anxious to get me out of town, even if it meant a delay in getting his ransom. Maybe it was an inflection in his voice, but I don't think he wants me to stay here, even though he can keep better tabs on my movements than if I'm in Seattle."

"If that's true, then why?" Jay pondered.

"Because you might discover where he's got David hidden," Carol answered.

"Maybe. Who, besides Maggie, hates me enough to do something like this?"

"Half the town."

"I'm not talking about just being angry because of something my father might've done," Jay said. "Those kinds of people wouldn't do more than paint on my car."

"Totally different modus operandi?"

"I see you read detective novels," he said deadpan. "Whoever did this are much more than anti-Semites."

"Couldn't it just be a kidnapping for profit?"

"Then, it was sure mounted quickly. Except for the people at the bank, nobody knew I was coming here."

"Why *not* somebody at the bank?"

"There's a lady there that doesn't seem to like me," Jay said. "I don't know why. But, nobody knew I was going to be there today until I walked through the door.

"Wait a minute!" He jumped up and began to pace again, his mind racing faster than the thoughts could flow from his mouth. "The same thing happened yesterday. Nobody knew I was going to stay here, yet Larry Palmer, or whatever his name was, called me right after I'd arrived. Today, I got a phone call in the bank. Who the hell's been following me?"

The blast of an auto horn delayed Carol's answer. She poked her head out the door. "I'll be back in a minute," she said to Jay. "Somebody's checking out."

"Can't Ralph handle it?"

"He's out doing some errands. Don't worry. This won't take long." She hurried out to attend to her business.

Jay checked his watch. It was nearly one. Another seven hours or so before it got dark and he could test his long shot theory. He was going to need Carol's assistance, but that didn't worry him. She seemed eager to help.

He was glad that he'd confided in her. By using her as a sounding board, the situation didn't seem as dark as it had before. She sparked his imagination and also came up with some useful observations herself. Thank God for her.

"Have you noticed any cars following you?" she asked as she reentered the cabin.

"No, but, then, I had no reason to look for any either."

She looked totally perplexed.

"Carol," he said, "the thing about the Storyman gave me an idea. I know it's a million-to-one shot, but right now that's all I got."

You don't think he's behind this, do you?"

"Of course not." Again, he paced about the cabin. "But, he could be a part of it. An innocent dupe."

"That's crazy! He's not capable of this sort of thing. Child molestation, maybe, but not kidnapping for ransom.

"Why are you eliminating Maggie?" she asked.

"Too slow and too obvious," Jay replied, temporarily dismissing the idea. He squatted next to her. "What if the brains behind this operation used O'Neil as bait to lure David into his car? Maybe the old man thought he was just going to tell the boy stories, show him a good time.

"Christ, I've told David a hundred times that he's not to talk to strangers."

"To Dave," she said, "the Storyman wasn't a stranger."

"Exactly!" Jay agreed. "O'Neil's shack out off the highway would be a perfect place to stash Dave. It's isolated. Nobody goes there. If the Storyman keeps him amused, Dave might not even know he's been kidnapped, at least not right away."

"You want to drive out there?"

"After it gets dark." He was glad that it was she who'd made the proposal. "I'm being watched, you know."

"I'm not," her eyes began to glisten. "We could take my station wagon. You hide in the back until we get away from here."

Jay was already miles ahead of her in his planning. Interesting how she echoed his thoughts. "I'll leave the light on in my cabin," he tendered. "With the Skylark still here, our 'friend' might not miss me."

Carol's excitement was suddenly gone. "This isn't going to work."

"Why?"

"We're talking like this is a television show. 'Mission Impossible,' or something. This is the real thing."

"Don't you think I know that?"

"What are we going to do if we find Dave out there? We could get our heads shot off."

"We're not going in with guns-a-blazin'," Jay said, trying to pacify her. "I don't even know how to use one."

"*So, what are we going to do?*" she insisted. "They're not going to let Dave go without a fight."

"You leave me there, then head for town and get the sheriff. While you're gone, I'll watch the place."

"What if they catch you?"

"I don't know," he said, not wanting to consider that possibility. "I'll just have to improvise."

EIGHT

"There's a car following us," Carol said. She headed her Dodge wagon east on Main.

Jay was on the floor of the back seat. He poked his head up for a look. A block behind them, two headlights were keeping pace. "Take a right, then gun it," he said.

She swung onto Second Street, cutting her lights and pressing down onto the gas. Jay kept watch through the back window. The vehicle in question continued up Main. "Forget it," he said. "False alarm."

Carol parked in front of one of the few houses on the block. "Let's wait here, just to be sure." They watched the road behind them. It was devoid of traffic.

"I'm wondering if my 'friend' was bluffing when he said he had a lot of accomplices," mused Jay.

"How's that?"

"Well, we don't seem to have been followed. Either you're very clever, or nobody was watching the court just now."

"I wouldn't get cocky just yet," remarked Carol. "I may be very clever."

"It also occurred to me this afternoon, when he called me at the service station, that he didn't say anything about my talk with LaGrange. I don't think he knew about it."

"What does that prove?"

"That I wasn't followed from the bank to the gas station. Maybe there're only two or three people in on this after all. One of them has to be watching David. The others keep tabs on me. They may not be watching me full time, just

92

cruising the court every now and then to see if the Skylark's still there."

"You could be right," Carol agreed, "but I'd still take it easy 'til I was sure."

She started the wagon and made a U-turn back to Main.

Jay had been waiting to take this ride all afternoon. The minutes had crawled by, particularly after Carol had left him alone in the cabin. She had chores to do, and she didn't want to upset her husband by spending too much time with this particular guest.

Two hours past. Bathed in sweat, Jay had stared at the walls, thinking of the precious moments he'd shared with David during the boy's five years. There was that first trip to Disneyland and the then three-year-old's speechless excitement at seeing Mickey Mouse in person, as well as his fright at Captain Hook. Then, there was the visit to the trout farm in the Malibu Mountains. When Dave caught his first fish and saw it twisting at the end of his line, he'd screamed, dropped the pole and run.

Jay refused to believe that he would never see his son again.

Somehow, around four-thirty, he'd dozed off. The tranquilizers, the heat and the day's events had reached him. It was not a restful sleep. He awakened suddenly at twenty-to-six, his head spinning. He had to get out of the cabin. The walls seemed to be closing in on him.

He drove into town, stopping at Al's cafe. Raspy Voice, after all, had given him permission to go out for meals twice-a-day. He didn't really feel hungry, but he ordered some soup and a tuna sandwich. To his surprise, he'd devoured it all.

When he got back to the trailer court at six-thirty, Carol had changed into slacks and a blouse. She greeted him with the news that Ed LaGrange had stopped by to pick him up.

"Oh, shit!" was Jay's reaction. "I forgot all about him. He invited me to dinner tonight."

"I covered for you as best I could," Carol said. "I told him you'd gotten an important call from Seattle and checked out."

"What did he say?"

"I think he was hurt, but what can you do?"

Jay was sorry about LaGrange, just as he'd felt bad about snubbing Chaney earlier in the day. Unfortunately, he couldn't rectify his bad manners right now. Etiquette was the least of his worries.

He'd paced the cabin for the next two hours, tried to sleep again, but couldn't. At eight-forty, Carol pulled her station wagon up next to the cabin door, parking in such a way as to obliterate a clear view from the street. Jay'd opened the vehicle's back door and crawled in onto the floor. He'd sat there as the car left the court.

"Why don't you come up front?" Carol suggested. She turned off Main onto the access road that led to the main highway. "I think it's clear now."

Jay climbed over the seat. "What did you tell Ralph?" he asked.

"I said we were going over to see Sam Jackson. I even asked if he wanted to come."

"What if he'd said 'Yes'?"

"He never goes anywhere with me, unless he has to."

"It's really none of my business," Jay offered, "but the two of you should get some sort of counseling. When I spoke to Ralph this morning, I got the impression there was a very tender man inside, crying for help."

For a moment, Jay thought she was going to cry. "I told you last night that he won't go for therapy."

Jay decided not to pursue the issue.

The sky was clear, allowing the half-moon to illuminate the otherwise dark highway. A few cars sped past the station wagon as it waited at the access road, each going toward some destination other than Mineral Lake. "I haven't been out here for years," Carol said. "Do you remember which way?"

"I think it's across the highway and up the road about a quarter mile."

She waited for a P.I.E. truck to go past, then moved swiftly across the thoroughfare. Neither of them saw the dip on the other side. The wagon hit hard, jarring its occupants. "Jesus!" Jay exclaimed. "I don't remember that one. You okay?"

"No broken teeth."

"You'd better kill the lights again. We don't want anyone to know we're coming."

"Wonderful," she smiled with an air of light sarcasm. "If we come to a cliff, we can go over in total ignorance." She cut the lights.

They moved slowly up the old wagon road, jostled by the multitude of bumps. The car windows were kept closed to avoid choking on the clouds of dust they were creating. There were no structures along the way, merely sagebrush and infinite desolation.

"Gee," quipped Carol, "I hope we can find our way back to the highway."

"There it is," said Jay. "Over to the right." The moonlight had enabled him to make out the dark forms of O'Neil's one room shack and the two story grape arbor standing next to it. The structures were about sixty yards off the road, flanked by a small orchard of five or six peach trees. The moon shining through it gave the arbor the appearance of a face wearing a grotesque smile.

Jay pointed to the shadow thrown by the trees. "Park here."

Carol retrieved a flashlight from the glove compartment. "How do you want to do this?"

"Why don't you wait in the car...."

"Bullshit!" she snapped. "You're not leaving me alone."

"But you'd be safer...."

"I'm going with you."

"Have it your way," Jay acquiesced. "We'll sneak over there and look around. If we find anything that looks promising, I'll stay and you go for the sheriff."

"You lead."

They stood by the car for a moment, listening. Somewhere in the distance, a dog barked. Otherwise, it was quiet, except for the familiar cricket serenade. Just like in the movies, Jay thought. Except when Eastwood or Redford went sneaking around, they didn't have to go to the bathroom.

He took the flashlight from Carol and trained its weak beam on the ground before them. "You could use some new batteries," he said.

Taking her hand, he moved forward, stepping cautiously onto the footpath leading to O'Neil's property. Rotting lumber, rusty gasoline cans, a ripped mattress and other debris were strewn along the way. Jay remembered that, in years past, the premises, though never elegant, had always been nicely kept. The Storyman had been proud of his property and had tried to maintain it for the children who visited.

No light was coming from the shanty. Jay could hear the ever faint sound of the radio. It was playing some obscure country tune. He motioned Carol to stand still. Again, they listened.

Somebody was shouting inside. The words were muffled by the music, yet there was definitely a man yelling.

Could he be shouting at David? Jay crept forward.

About twenty feet from the decaying structure, he nearly stumbled over the picket fence that surrounded the nucleus of the property. Much of the once sturdy wooden barrier had been knocked down and was covered with brush.

"Sons-of-bitches!" the voice inside shouted. "Dirty sons-of-bitches!"

The trespassers maneuvered their way through the open gate, careful to avoid the fence. "Wait here," Jay whispered. "I'm going to take a peek."

Jay hurried over to the shack's sole window, stepping gingerly onto a small wooden crate just below it. Carol remained at the gate, primed to sprint back to the car upon Jay's command.

"Dirty bastards!" Jay recognized the voice now as being O'Neil's. "Miserable sons-of-bitches! I jest wanted to play with their babies."

Jay peered through the cracked glass. It was totally dark inside. He could make out no shapes. The sound of O'Neil's voice moved around the shack, as if the old man were pacing about.

Barnett listened more intently, hoping to hear the voice or whimper of a child; *David's* voice or whimper.

A dog growled from within. Nothing else. Only the Storyman's ramblings and the creaking of the floorboards as he moved back and forth. Jay began to think this jaunt might be a waste of time.

O'Neil's wrinkled face was suddenly at the window; his tired eyes staring directly into Jay's. Moonlight reflected off the features, whitening them into a ghostly mask.

"*Jesus Christ!*" Startled, Jay stepped backwards, tumbling off the box onto the hard ground. He scrambled to his feet and, ignoring his sore buttocks, ran toward Carol, who'd moved to the outer side of the gate.

"What was it?" she asked in a loud whisper.

Jay hadn't time to reply. O'Neil was on the porch, shining a flashlight in his direction. The torch was blinding. "Get 'em, Rex!" he shouted.

A large dog, possibly a German Shepherd, lunged in Jay's direction, barking viciously. *Run, Carol,* Jay yelled. She made a dash for the road. He tried to follow, but tripped over the reclining fence.

The dog was closing the distance between them. Jay grasped a rock. He flung it at the animal. Missed. The beast kept coming.

The station wagon was too far. That snarling beast would be upon him before he was halfway there. Better to try for the grape arbor by the house.

Grabbing a loose board, Jay got to his feet just as Rex was about to spring. There was no time to get a firm hold on the wood. He jabbed at the animal, hitting it on the chest.   It gave out with a yelp as it lost its balance.

Jay didn't wait for Rex to recover. Faster than he'd ever run before, he covered the span to the arbor and, with one large leap, grasped the trellis about halfway to the top. Already the dog was nipping at his heels. He scurried higher, until he was out of Rex's reach. The Shepherd's front legs were on the latticework, his teeth bared at his treed quarry.

What the hell was he going to do now, Jay wondered.

"What're you doin' here?" O'Neil was standing by the arbor, shining his bright light up at him.

"Hi, Mr. O'Neil." Jay tried to appear calm, even though the creaking wood made him fearful that the trellis was not going to support him much longer. He figured there must be a hundred splinters in his hands.

"Who are you?" O'Neil demanded.

"Jay Barnett. Harry Barnett's son. Remember? I picked you up on the road yesterday. I had my boy, David, with me."

"Oh, sure. I remember you. How's yer father these days?"

"He's dead." Jay didn't think he could hang on much longer, but Rex was still snarling.

"Somebody told me that," O'Neil reflected. "I don't remember who."

"Mr. O'Neil, do you mind if I come down?"

"Come ahead."

"Would you please call off your dog?"

"Rex, stay!" the oldster commanded. The dog retreated to his master's side and sat, ears alert.

Barnett hesitated until he was sure of the animal. He climbed down slowly, careful not to press his damaged hands against the hard wood.

The Storyman looked at Jay, waiting for some explanation for his presence. What was he going to tell the old geezer? Based on O'Neil's attitude and the lack of any evidence that David was there, Jay was certain that his earlier suspicions were unjustified. He felt embarrassed.

"We were driving by," he ad-libbed, "and we thought we'd drop in." O'Neil didn't respond. He stared at him with a blank expression. "I heard voices inside, so I looked in the window. I didn't want to bother you if you had company."

"Where's the little boy that were with ya yesterday?"

"He's home asleep."

"Why don't ya bring him tomorrow? I'd like to see him again."

"Well, sure...."

O'Neil appeared to be talking in a daze. "I won't hurt him. Those things those people said about me weren't true. I didn't do nothing to their boy. He were a good kid."

"I never believed a word of it," Jay answered, feeling great pity for the old man.

"You bring yer boy tomorrow," the Storyman said, a gleam appearing in his eye. "I'll show him a good time. I'll be nice to him."

"I'll try." Jay started to walk away. It was a waste of time to stay here. O'Neil obviously knew nothing about David's whereabouts. "You, by any chance, didn't happen to see my boy today?" he asked, knowing the answer would be negative.

"He ain't been around for a couple of weeks."

"Thank you," Jay said, not wanting to contend with O'Neil's senility. He headed back toward the road. O'Neil and his dog, tail wagging, watched him go, then went back into the shack.

"Are you okay?" Carol was standing next to the wagon. "I didn't know what to do. I started to go for help...."

"I'm fine," Jay said. "My hands are a little battered, but otherwise...."

"What happened?"

"Nothing. A goddamn wild goose chase." He slid into the car on the passenger side. "You know, I've never been more frightened in my life. I thought that fucking dog was going to kill me."

"I was scared, too," she said, starting the engine. "I was bit by a dog when I was seven. It isn't fun."

"I still can't believe all this is happening."

"How are your hands?" The car was turned around and heading back toward the highway.

"Full of splinters. You got a needle or something?"

"A sewing kit's in my purse. Let's go back home and I'll dig them out for you."

"Christ, no!!" he replied. "I've been in that damn cabin all day. Let's go for a drive. Maybe I can think better. Come up with a less far-fetched idea."

"There's a small rocky beach on the other side of the lake. We can go there, and, while you hold the flashlight, I'll play Florence Nightingale."

"Good idea." He gazed out the window into the darkness, wondering what in the world he was going to do next.

Claude Bates was locking up the Texaco station when he saw the station wagon turn onto the road that ran along the lake. He recognized the man and woman inside the vehicle immediately. His curiosity aroused, he headed for his battered white pick-up. This looked like the perfect opportunity to get even with that "stuck-up Jew bastard."

NINE

"Hold your hand still and I'll get it."

Jay grimaced as Carol worked the needle in under the splinter. "Careful. It hurts." He moved the light in closer.

"Don't be such a baby. This is the last one."

He averted his eyes from her minor surgery; looked out at the waves lapping up onto the rocks, leaving a residue of suds. Three miles in the distance, he could see lights from Mineral Lake. Funny, in all the summers he'd lived here, Jay had never visited this little out-of-the-way beach. Here it was, only a few feet off the lake shore road, and he didn't even know it existed.

"Got it!" Carol announced. "That'll be ten dollars, please."

Jay flexed his hands. They were sore from her digging. She'd removed fourteen of those damn slivers. He slid out of the wagon, walked down to the water and stuck in his hands. The cold liquid stung the wounds, but he kept them immersed. Mineral Lake would heal the cuts and prevent infection.

"Beats iodine every time." Carol sat on the ground next to him. "Better?"

"They will be," Jay said. He splashed some cool water on his perspiring face, then grabbed a handkerchief from his back pocket and wiped his hands. "Do you remember Toby, the cocker spaniel?"

"Can't say that I do."

"He made *Newsweek*. The mutt had a whole paragraph written about him. Remember? He was the dog that got hit by the car and had his front leg amputated." Carol shook her head. She still didn't know what he was talking about.

"The stump got infected," he continued, "and the vet said the dog might have to be destroyed. Then, all of a sudden, the infection started to clear up. Toby was taking swims in the lake and the water cured him.

"My dad learned about the dog and thought his story would be great promotion for the town. He wrote to the magazine and they printed it."

"I never heard about that," she said.

"Dad was always trying to ballyhoo this place. He even had some big motel chain, Travelodge or one of those, interested in putting up a new motel on our property. They'd have built a nice restaurant, some shops. It would've really upgraded the town."

"Please, Jay," Carol said, "I know the whole story of how Maggie blocked their getting the building permits and licenses."

Barnett smiled. "I guess I lose track of how often I tell it." He lay back onto the gravel, propping himself up onto his elbows. "I was working up to saying how nuts the people are here. I got virtually a whole town that hates me because my father quit them. They forget that they're the ones that turned on him."

"They voted Maggie out of office, didn't they?" She gently ran her finger along his arm. He didn't respond.

"Sure," he said, "a couple of years later. After he'd lost interest in this place. Hell, do you know how many sickies you've got here? Forget about the people who are just plain rude. You've got somebody running around who committed a murder years ago, there's a few bigots that paint 'nice' sayings on cars, kidnappers, arsonists...." He thought of adding "drunks." He decided he shouldn't.

"What arsonists?" She halted her caresses.

"I don't know. I just threw it in to make my list longer. Something happened last night. I'm not sure if I dreamt it or not." He told her about the man he'd thought had tried to enter his cabin and the lingering smell of gasoline in the air.

"Maybe what you smelled came from the street," she suggested.

"The experience seemed too real to have completely been my imagination. Maybe somebody just walked by my cabin and I only thought he was trying to get inside."

"Of course," Carol said hesitantly. "That could be it. I'm sure there's a less ominous explanation. There can't be that many people in town who are out to get you."

"I hope." He put his hands under his head and looked up at the stars. It seemed impossible to relax. The muggy air around them didn't help. "Carol," he said, "where are we going to look for David?"

"I'd go to the law," she said. "I could call them from Ephrata."

"Forget it! How's the F.B.I. going to operate undercover in a town the size of Mineral Lake? Any other ideas?"

"I keep thinking that Maggie might have something to do with it."

"She's too old and her son is too delicate."

"I'm not necessarily saying they did it alone. Remember the logistics. David disappeared from the play yard adjoining the hotel. While your back was turned, they could have pulled him inside the building. How long would that have taken?"

Jay sat up and looked at her. "I never thought of that. But, who could've helped them?"

"How much strength does it take to grab a five-year-old?"

"You don't know David. He's pretty feisty."

"Maybe they lured him inside. Maggie could've done that herself. All I'm saying is, the hotel would have been an excellent place to hide him. He might even still be there."

Barnett was on his feet, heading back to the car. "What are we waiting for? Let's go down there."

She grabbed his arm. "This isn't the same as going out into the toolies somewhere and spying on a senile old man. There's too many people around the hotel."

"We'll be more careful," he said. If David is at the hotel, I'm going to find out *now*. Do you drive, or do I?"

"Jay," she said, maintaining her grip on his arm, "Maggie has over twenty rooms in that dump. Most of them are occupied. You can't go busting in there without some advance planning. Unless, of course, you want your kidnapper 'friend' to know you're out and about."

"What do you suggest?" he asked, suppressing his anger.

"Tomorrow, I'll go...."

"Tomorrow!" he shouted. "Are you crazy? They could move him by then. If David is down there, I'm getting him out tonight!"

"And, if he's not, then what do you do?" He didn't respond. "First of all, they'd be foolish to move him out of the hotel. It's safer to leave him locked up in an empty room."

A picture of the boy, tied to a bedpost, flashed through Jay's head.

Carol continued. "I'll go down there and lay some groundwork. I'll butter Maggie up a bit, try to find out which rooms are vacant, who's staying there...."

"You can't do that now?"

"It's nearly midnight."

"What happens after you go down there?"

"If I think there's anything suspicious going on, we'll go back tomorrow night and look the place over. But, at least, we'll have an idea where to look."

"That's nearly twenty-four hours from now," he muttered.

"You said yourself that David would be okay until you dropped off the ransom. You're going to get him back safely. I'm sure of that.

"We'd better get home," she said, opening the door to the wagon. "I don't want to upset Ralph again."

Jay was back in the rear seat as Carol turned onto the lake shore route, heading in the direction of town. No other cars were traveling on the narrow curve-ridden course. She proceeded cautiously, straddling the center of the road, keeping alert for the few fluorescent markers painted on the cliff walls.

"Somehow it's always easier coming from the other direction than driving back," she said. The wagon was creeping at twenty-five.

"You should try driving through mountains at night in a rainstorm." Jay glanced out the back window. About two hundred yards behind them, a pair of high beam headlights flashed, vanished around a bend, then appeared again. The vehicle was moving up fast. "Looks like somebody wants to live dangerously," he commented.

Carol peered at the rearview mirror. "That's stupid, driving that way on this road."

Jay studied the lights as they jumped back-and-forth around the curves, increasing in size each time they returned to view. He wondered if the screwy driver would see the wagon in time to apply his brakes.

"I hope we don't get rear-ended," Carol verbalized his thought. She increased her speed slightly, struggling with the wheel to negotiate the hooks in the road. "This car was not built for racing."

The lights were drawing closer. Fifty yards now. Before they disappeared again, the moonlight gave Jay a glimpse of the vehicle, a light colored pick-up truck. "This guy is going to be on top of us in a minute." He remembered the turn-out he'd utilized earlier in the day. The strip was at least a half mile away. "There's a spot up here aways where you can pull over and let this freak pass," he said, not taking his eyes off the road behind him.

Only a half dozen car lengths were separating the two vehicles. The pick-up began honking, first in short bursts, then in one steady wail. The driver refused to reduce his speed. Carol pressed down further on the gas, but the truck didn't allow her to increase the distance between them. "What's that schmuck trying to do?" Jay wondered.

The pick-up was right on the wagon's tail. Its blinding light shown through the window. Jay had to look away. Carol found it impossible to check her rearview mirror.

"He's going to ram us," Jay shouted. He braced himself against the seat.

They felt the first impact almost as he finished speaking. Jay was propelled forward, then, as Carol swerved away from the rock wall, he was thrown to the floor. Wedged between the seats, he hit his head as the truck struck again. This time, the wagon came within inches of the wall before Carol righted it.

Who was this guy, Jay tried to figure. Could it be the kidnapper trying to teach him a lesson? He grasped the seat and pulled himself up. The lights prevented him from even seeing the truck, let alone the driver. Another impact. he went sprawling.

"The guy's nuts!" yelled Jay.

Again the pick-up attacked. The jolt caused Carol to momentarily lose command of the wheel. The wagon veered toward the guardrail. She recovered quickly and twisted the control sharply to the left. Jay saw the sparks and heard the scraping as the vehicle's front bumper bounced against the wall.

Were they going to end up in flames like Jerry Roscoe? Jay felt like a lobster suspended over a pot of boiling water.

Carol was maintaining her cool. She gripped the wheel tightly, her eyes searching for the turn-out up ahead. As the wagon rounded an outward hook, she noted that the truck had drifted back slightly. The driver was trying to achieve more force with the next thrust. "Hold on!" she shouted to Jay, who was sitting up again.

At the far side of the curve, she slammed on her brakes, twisting the wheel sharply to the left. Jay fell backward onto the seat. The rear end of the wagon spun in a counter-clockwise direction until it had completed almost a one hundred-eighty-degree arc. It stopped, facing back in the opposite direction.

The driver of the truck veered quickly to the right in an effort to avoid a head-on collision. Traveling so fast, he lost control, skimming over the thin turn-out and through the flimsy guardrail beyond. Shaken, Jay and Carol watched with disbelief as the vehicle hit the rocky bank, flipped over, then plunged into the blackness that was Mineral Lake.

"He bailed out the window," Jay said, bounding over to where the truck had gone through the railing. Carol followed with the flashlight. The bank was only five feet high at this spot. They watched the upturned vehicle sink below the water's surface, one light still shining brightly.

The driver swam toward them. He was gasping for breath and blood appeared to be pouring from a cut on his forehead. It was Claude Bates. Jay picked up a large rock, prepared to crown him.

Bates' hands searched for a spot on shore to grasp. "Please help me!" He choked on the words.

"Get up here, you bastard," Jay yelled. He flung the rock down at Bates. It hit a boulder next to the injured man and ricocheted into the lake.

Claude looked up at him. His eyes rolled upward. He slid back into the water.

As much as he wanted to, Jay knew he couldn't let Bates drown, even if such a thing were possible in Mineral Lake. He wanted the son-of-a-bitch dead; but, then, he had to live with himself. On the other hand, perhaps Bates was part of the kidnapping plot and, in his weakened state, would be primed to talk.

Grabbing hold of a dangling cable from the razed guardrail, Barnett worked his way down the rocks until he was a foot above the waterline. Carol pointed the flashlight beam ahead of him. "Take my hand, asshole!" Jay shouted to Bates, who, though afloat, was having problems keeping his face out of the water.

Bates reached out his hand and Jay seized it, pulling the injured man halfway up onto the bank. He lay there, panting. Jay sat on a boulder just above him. "Any bones broken?" he asked, half hoping the answer would be affirmative.

"I don't think so," the attendant answered. "But, my head hurts. It hurts like hell!"

"Good!" Jay grabbed his hair and pulled it hard. His cuts appeared to be superficial. "You're going to have a beautiful scar, Claude," Jay said, "but you'll live. Now, where's my kid?"

"Huh?"

"Tell me or I'll push you back in and hold your head under."

"I don't know nuthin' about your kid" Bates appeared totally bewildered.

Carol had worked her way down the bank to join Jay. "I don't think he knows," she whispered into his ear. "Why did you do this?" she asked the attendant.

No answer.

Jay cocked his fist. "Tell her!"

"This morning…," Claude sobbed, "I wanted to get you for what you did to me."

"Liar!"

"No, I swear that's the truth."

Barnett had to believe him. As much as he wanted Claude to be part of the plot, this was the more logical motive. He had, after all, given Bates quite a beating. "Are you sure somebody else didn't put you up to this?"

"Nobody did. I saw you drive out here, that's all."

Using the cable, Jay started to pull himself back up to where Carol was standing, shining her light on Claude. "Have a nice walk back to town," he said to Bates.

"If he's badly hurt and we don't get him medical attention," Carol cautioned, "we could be in real trouble." She flashed her light on the superficial damage to the rear bumper and left front fender of her station wagon.

Barnett knew she was right again. "Come on, asshole," he called. "We'll take you to the hospital."

The only sounds inside the station wagon as it headed back into town were Bates' occasional sobs and his chattering teeth. He huddled on the floor in the back seat while Jay, sitting across from him, restrained himself from kicking the little prick in the head.

Carol turned the car into the driveway of the Mason Hospital and proceeded to the emergency entrance. Through the glass door, they could see the sole resident physician on duty. He was sitting in the waiting room, reading a magazine. It appeared to be a slow evening.

"What about my truck?" Bates asked as he got out of the wagon. His old surliness was returning.

Jay knew there was nothing seriously wrong with him. "You *must* be kidding," he chuckled. Carol joined him in the guffaw.

"You wrecked my truck!" Bates persisted, his tone becoming angrier.

"You damaged my station wagon," Carol said, still amused.

"Claude," Jay said, "you forget about this morning, and we'll forget that you tried to kill us. If anybody asks, you ran your truck off the road all by yourself."

The station wagon headed toward the court. "You were great out there, Spunky," Jay said, sliding down onto the floor of the back seat. "Where'd you learn to drive like that?"

"I've seen *The French Connection* five times."

"Who says movies don't have an educational value?" He leaned his head back and tried to flush everything from his mind. Only the vision of his frightened child remained.

From his bedroom window, Chaney watched his station wagon stop in front of Cabin Two. The rear door on the far side opened, and Barnett got out. He gave Carol a slight wave, then went inside the well-lit cottage.

Chaney gulped some more liquid from his glass. That call he'd just received had been very enlightening. It had confirmed his suspicions. He took his .45 automatic from his top dresser drawer and began rubbing it with an oil cloth.

TEN

David screamed. A tall, faceless phantom in a black shroud held him over the edge of Dead Man's Bluff.

Jay tried to reach him, but something was holding him back. Frantically, he looked about for help.

He spotted somebody. A familiar face. Jerry Roscoe. There were tears in Jerry's eyes.

"Daddy!" David screamed.

Jay awoke disoriented, drenched in sweat. He tried to recall the nightmare he'd just experienced, but the details remained vague.

The strenuous events of last night had been so exhausting, he'd fallen asleep with his clothes on. Sleep had been an off-and-on affair. Now, eight hours later, he felt hung over; hardly rested at all.

David had been gone for nearly twenty-four hours. The thought lay like a rock in his gut.

He stripped off his shirt and used it to wipe the perspiration from his body. If he was going to be stuck in this damn oven another day, he'd better get an electric fan or something.

He peered through the window. Aside from a blue Chevy van going past, Fourth Street was empty. Par for a Saturday morning in Mineral Lake.

A long shower made him slightly more comfortable. He dressed quickly, donning polished cottons and a fresh sport shirt. Now, what?

It was nearly nine. If he went out to breakfast right away, then he'd have to stay here until dinner time with nothing to occupy himself but counting knotholes. Maybe it would be better if he waited until later; break up the tedium more. Raspy voice never said when he had to go to breakfast.

He thought again of David and the dream; wondered if his son was being well fed. If the kidnappers had any smarts at all, he rationalized, they'd try to be gentle with him. Terrorizing the boy would only make him cry and retreat within himself. No, they had to be intelligent enough to know that, with kindness, they would get him to be more cooperative to their demands. He prayed he was right.

Carol had said that she'd go down to see Maggie about noon. The old gal was usually in the lobby then and Carol could just be "passing by." He'd agreed with her that she should try to make it a "casual" meeting. That way, Maggie would be less on guard.

The four hours or so before Carol would give him her report promised to be intolerable.

He decided to think about something else. The movie! *Repercussions*. How was he going to get it out of hock?

He'd been able to get it made by breaking the first rule of movie-making.

He'd financed it with his own money.
Schmuck!

But, nobody else was handing him the dough. After months of soul searching and sleepless nights, he'd decided to gamble on himself.

Jay had mortgaged virtually everything he owned, then called in favors from actors and various behind-the-scenes professionals that he'd dealt with over the years. Surprisingly, almost everybody he asked had agreed to work for scale and in most cases, even defer that minimum salary until the film was sold.

They did it because they liked him, but, more importantly, they liked his script. He'd written a damn good one...and people in Hollywood always wanted to be associated with a hit.

Getting a cast and much of his crew to work on the cuff was only half the battle. He still had to buy film, rent equipment and pay all the other production and post-production costs involved in the making of the film, such as music scoring and sound recording.

That's the part that really put him into hock.

As is so often their custom with low budget filmmakers, the lab had agreed to defer their processing charges, but now their deadline was quickly approaching and they wanted their money.

Maybe if he called the business affairs guy at the lab.... What was his name? Meyer Dolinsky. That was it. He seemed like a nice guy. If he explained to him what had happened, maybe Dolinsky would give him more time before he foreclosed on the negative and put it up for auction.

Maybe he would even be sympathetic enough to extend a little more credit and run him off a color-corrected print, so that he could show it around to distributors, or enter it in a film festival or two.

He knew he had a winner with this picture...if he could just get it seen.

Jay suddenly felt guilty that he was thinking about the movie, and not his son. "What's the matter with me?" he asked aloud.

He grabbed a yellow legal pad out of his attache´ case and sat back on the bed. Strange how problems always seemed to be simplified when they were reduced to paper. At the top of the page, he wrote "People Who Hate Me Enough." He smiled to himself, thinking how much fun his shrink could have with that paranoid heading.

First on his list was "Maggie Murphy and son," followed by "Claude Bates," and "teller at bank." That sourpuss had something stuck in her craw. He remembered the man at the Mineral Lake Grill who'd been glowering at him and added him to the tally.

Who else might be a suspect?

A catch-all listing: "People Who Think Dad Ruined Them."

Who else?

He started to cross out Bates' name. If he was involved in this plot, surely some hint would have been dropped last night. Claude was too much of a simpleton to be able to conceal something like that. On the other hand, why let the schmuck off the hook so easily. He let Bates stay and wrote "Ralph Chaney."

Carol's husband was a long shot, but certainly worth considering. The jealousy factor gave him a motive of sorts. Also, on the day Barnett had arrived in town, couldn't Chaney have alerted "Larry Palmer" as to his whereabouts while Jay was talking with Carol? Logistically, it was possible, however remote.

Barnett studied the roster for a while, then added another entry: "People Who Owed Dad Money."

He really needed Alan's help on that category. When the Barnett estate had been divided, Jay had taken the stocks, bonds and remaining Mineral Lake real estate, while his brother had laid claim to, among other items, trust deeds and notes. As Jay remembered, Alan had had some problems collecting on a couple of those pieces of paper. He'd applied pressure. Perhaps some of those debtors bore grudges. Jay wouldn't know until he spoke to Alan.

He wondered if this avenue was really viable enough to risk making a call to Seattle. If the kidnappers found out, that could be the ball game.

He tossed the pad onto the other bed. This was stupid! There were dozens of people with motives. Without a substantial lead of some sort, this was all mental masturbation. Jesus, he hoped that Carol would come up with something this afternoon.

His stomach began talking to him. It was after ten. He decided to drive over to Al's.

Breakfast was in full swing when Jay parked in front of the eatery. An indistinguishable array of the local citizenry occupied almost every stool and booth. He chose to wait in his air-conditioned car until the place emptied out a bit.

Jay gazed over at the print shop next door. He'd forgotten about Sam these past twenty-four hours. Jackson could be a big help to him. In fact, he'd be eager to assist. Sam knew everybody and everything in this town; the gossip, the grudges, the screwballs. His knowledge could be the key to the crucial lead he needed to see that David was returned safely.

But, how to get to him? The ex-editor's office was just a few feet away. It would be so easy to cross that bit of pavement and turn the door handle.

What if the kidnapper was watching? He most likely was. That short walk could prove disastrous.

Maybe Carol might act as an intermediary; find a way to get the two of them together in a clandestine meeting. He'd speak to her about it.

Jackson's account of the Mineral Lake murder suddenly came to mind. What a time to be dwelling on such trivia, he scolded himself. Nevertheless, there was something about the case that was so familiar. His parents hadn't told him anything about it. He was sure of that. No, it reminded him of a movie he'd seen.

The title and cast of the film eluded him. They were nearly within his mental grasp, but just when he thought he had it, the picture was gone. It was an old mystery movie, set in a small rural village. There were swamps with mists, British accents, and a ghostly phantom running around ripping out people's throats.

Damn! What was the name of that turkey?

"I want to talk to you." Sheriff LaGrange pulled open the door of the Skylark and waited for Jay to step out. There was anger in his eyes.

"Oh, hi, Ed...." Jay exhibited a weak smile, fumbling for an explanation for his rude behavior the previous night. That they were probably being watched, made the task even more difficult.

He wished it were possible to confide in LaGrange.

"You're no better than yer smart-assed brother," interrupted the lawman, his voice low and tense. Just because you were born rich, that don't mean you can kick somebody in the face."

"I can explain about last night. It was...."

"I don't want yer goddamn excuses. My wife has no use for you Barnetts, but I insisted she go out and buy a roast. You see, I had a lot of respect for yer father. He was a gentleman to me. But, you two brats are somethin' else...."

It was Jay's turn to interrupt. "You lost me back there. What do you have against my brother?"

"You know what he did."

"I have no idea."

"Yer dad loaned me five thousand dollars years ago. After he died, I fell a couple months behind on the payments and yer brother started putting the screws on. I had to go out and refinance my house at a higher interest rate to pay him off."

Barnett summoned to mind the list he'd made earlier: "People Who Owed Dad Money." Was LaGrange the kidnapper's entree to the sheriff's office?

"That had nothing to do with me," Jay said, taking the offensive. "Alan took over all of Dad's notes."

"I know that, but...."

"And, as for yesterday, something urgent came up." Jay recalled Carol's lie. "I had to leave town for the night. I'm sorry. I just forgot to phone you."

"My wife really went to a lot of trouble...."

"Please apologize to her for me. I'll even send over some flowers if it'll make her feel better."

LaGrange stared at him, trying to find a reasonable path through which he could vent his still viable anger. "Don't bother," he snapped. He stalked over to his car. "I wish I'd ticketed you."

"Fuck you!" Jay muttered, watching him drive off. "I got troubles enough."

He slid into an empty booth in the rear of the restaurant. The place was now only a quarter full. Two men were at the counter. The younger was tall, muscle-bound, in his early twenties. The other was of average build. With their hawk-like noses and deep-set eyes, they bore a strong resemblance to each other; probably father and son.

Jay recognized the older man. He was the middle-aged guy who had glowered at him in the Grill the other night. He was still glowering.

Barnett flashed a silly grin at the character, got no reaction, then picked up a copy of the *Seattle Times* which a previous customer had left on the table. He called his order of steak and eggs to the little blonde school girl behind the counter, and turned to the entertainment pages.

Halfway through the meal, Jay looked up to see the older gent sit across from him. The expression on his face said he wanted to fight. The younger version remained at the counter, his eyes trained on them.

"Something I can do for you?" Barnett asked, trying to appear nonchalant. He pretended to be involved with the paper.

"How can you sit there and not feel any guilt?" the man asked in a rough-edged voice that reminded Jay of George C. Scott.

He could see that he was in for another "hate Barnett" speech, and this one promised much more rancor than had been spit out by LaGrange. "Come again?"

"Do you know what your family has done to me? How they destroyed my life?"

Jay had no answer. He wanted to get up and leave. Over at the counter, the young man's eyes telegraphed that that would not be a wise move. The boy looked mean. Jay stuck a piece of meat into his mouth and forced himself to swallow.

"I had a nice business," the man continued, his ire building. "I wasn't rich, but I made a decent living. Enough to take care of my family an'...."

"Look, Mr...?"

"Farnsworth. Bill Farnsworth."

"Mr. Farnsworth," Jay said, "I know what you're leading up to. I'm sorry. I'm not responsible for my father's acts."

"Somebody has to be!" Farnsworth was shouting. "He killed the tourist trade. I depended on that."

"Mr. Farnsworth...." Jay tried to soothe the man whose eyes now bulged with hate.

"Don't humor me!"

"I'm not trying to humor you, sir." He could see that Farnsworth had probably waited years to blow off steam at a Barnett. *Any* Barnett.

"Then listen!" Farnsworth demanded. "The tourists stopped coming here, and the business I worked my ass off to build went down the tubes. Our savings were lost. My boy over there had to forget about college...."

"And we Jews crucified Christ, too," barked Jay, hoping to throw his antagonist off guard.

He'd had enough of this shit. He grabbed his check and walked over to the cash register, pretending not to see "Junior" Farnsworth, who stood up, looking to his father for instructions.

"Don't you walk out on me!" The older man was out of the booth and on Jay's heels. "You owe me, Barnett!"

"Bug off, mister." Jay tried to sound tough. He exited the eatery, heading for his car. He knew the Farnsworths were ready to explode, but he tried not to show his fear. If he could only get inside his vehicle before....

"Don't talk to my father like that." Jay felt Junior's huge paw clamp down onto his shoulder. Before he could speak, he was spun around to face the two men.

"If you hit me, I'll have you arrested for assault and battery," he gulped. The Farnsworths either didn't hear him or didn't care. Jay felt his legs go weak. "I've done nothing wrong to you."

Barnett saw the father start to bring his knee up, then felt a sharp pain in the groin. He doubled over. Junior grabbed his shirt front, straightening him up again. The young Farnsworth slapped him full force across the face. Jay fell back over the hood of the car. His ears were ringing, and his face burned.

"More Dad? Should I give him more?" Junior grabbed Jay's arm and started pulling him to his feet.

"Naw, don't hurt 'im. He might call the sheriff." His tone was mocking. He motioned for his son to stand back, so that he could face Jay. Barnett sat on the hood, his head in his hands. "Look at me, you son-of-a-bitch!"

Jay raised his head. He was too dazed; in too much pain to run. He saw the elder Farnsworth standing there, yet his words seemed to be coming through an echo chamber.

"I don't know why you came back here, or what you're after," Farnsworth said, "but we don't want you here. You understand?"

Jay nodded. He saw the man pucker his lips. A mass of sputum shot from his mouth, hitting him between the eyes.

"Now you know what we think about you Barnetts." The Farnsworths stalked off without looking back.

At that moment, Jay hated his father. He mentally cursed his memory. Why must he be made to suffer for Harry's acts? It wasn't fair.

And, this goddamn town. How dare they treat him like shit. He wished he had a torch. He'd set fire to the whole fucking place.

He wiped the spittle from his face, looking at the handkerchief to make sure there was no blood. They'd been wise. They'd struck no area that would bleed. Within a few minutes, the redness from Junior's slap would be gone. How could he convince the law that he'd been attacked?

The young waitress and a couple of male patrons from Al's stood in the doorway. They'd seen everything. The men's eyes appeared to be laughing at him. Somewhere, a phone rang.

Goddamn! He wanted to leave this place. Just give him back his boy and he'd go. Fuck the land deal! That could be finished by mail.

He wished for a baseball bat. He'd go after the Farnsworths right now and knock their heads off. He wasn't going to let them get away with this. No way would they walk away clean.

Suddenly, he realized what he was doing. More than likely, Claude Bates had said the same thing about him yesterday. The comparison was denigrating.

"You're Mr. Barnett, aren't you?" The waitress was at his side. Jay looked at her. He didn't speak. "There's a phone call for you."

Knowing that the caller was likely to be Raspy Voice, brought Jay to full alertness. He raced to the wall phone in the back of the restaurant. "Yes?" he said into the receiver.

"What were you doing with the sheriff?" the kidnapper said. "Didn't I warn you...?"

"I didn't invite him to talk to me," Jay answered, not hiding his anger. He glanced out the window. From where had the caller or his confederate been watching him?

"What did you tell him?"

"Nothing." He tried to keep his voice low. "In fact, I was rude to him. Look, when can I talk to David?"

Raspy Voice ignored the question. "Don't fuck with me, Barnett. I'll find out what you told LaGrange."

"I'm doing everything you've said. I just had breakfast, and I'm heading back to my cabin. Now, what about David?"

"There's a double-barrel shotgun right next to me. If I even think you're being bad, I'll blast the kid's head off."

Jay heard the familiar click of the phone. He cursed as he slammed the receiver down into its cradle.

The waitress was back behind the counter. The patrons had returned to their meals. All were pretending not to see him.

A feeling of nausea swept through Jay. He fled from the restaurant. Outside, he stopped and deposited his breakfast onto the sidewalk.

ELEVEN

Carol Franklin Chaney ran her finger around the rim of her coffee mug and procrastinated whether she should walk over to the counter to pour herself another refill. She'd been sitting at her kitchen table for nearly an hour, looking at the *Grant County Ledger*, yet not really reading it. It was almost noon. The thought of what she had to do turned her stomach.

She was dumb to have involved herself in this thing. Stupid! Stupid! Stupid!

Jay should have called in the authorities immediately. They were better equipped to handle incidents like this. Some way could be found to contact them without the kidnappers finding out.

My God! She'd almost been killed last night.

She owed Jay nothing. Sure, they'd made love a long time ago. No, "fucked" was a better word for it. They were awkward little virgins then. Neither knew what they were doing. It was just one step beyond playing "doctor." And, did she thank God when her period came along three weeks later.

Twice she'd written him after they'd returned to their home towns. He'd never answered. She'd felt cheap. Used. For a couple of years, she'd even hated him, until a few boyfriends later, she realized that Jay wasn't so different from most guys. Affection scared the shit out of them. She'd simply expected more from Jay at fifteen than he was able to give.

Too bad they didn't meet a few years later. Things might have been different.

The marriage to Ralph had been a shotgun affair. So many Yakima weddings were. She'd loved him though, ever since high school, and, for a time, she thought he felt the same way toward her.

He had been the star center and captain of the basketball team, and she was a cheer leader, pom-poms and all. Neither one were "A" pupils, but they were, nevertheless, the school's "First Couple," walking to class every day hand-in-hand, the envy of every romantic-minded student on campus.

Ralph had hoped to get a basketball scholarship to the University of Washington, but when that didn't happen and she became pregnant the summer after graduation, the only course of action in their small community was a quick wedding…followed, a few months later, by a "premature birth".

He got a "management trainee" job at the local supermarket, and, subsidized by their parents, they moved into a small house off of Main Street.

They had their problems, sure, but they made the best of it and were reasonably happy. She was wise enough not to object when he went to play basketball with the guys two nights a week, while she stayed home and took care of baby Randy. Ralph *loved* basketball.

One night, he'd come home and announced that he'd joined the Army. He had a wife and child. He could've gotten a deferment…but *he'd enlisted*.

"I'm an American," he told her. "It's my patriotic duty."

They had a huge fight that evening. "Bull!" she'd barked at him. "You just want to get away from me and Randy."

"That's a lie!" he'd yelled back, cocking his fist at her.

She'd stood her ground, daring him to hit her. Instead, he'd stormed out of the house. It was after midnight when he'd staggered back, totally soused, and passed out on the living room couch.

Two days later, he'd brought home flowers… carnations and roses. She loved roses. They made up…somewhat. After all, married people were supposed to fight and make up, weren't they? That's what her parents did.

Strange how he'd acted when she'd come in last night. He'd been drinking, which was nothing new, however, instead of the verbal jabs she'd come to expect, he'd been very sweet...passive.

Even when she lied, telling him how the station wagon had been damaged by a hit-and-run driver, he'd been quiet for a few moments, then without much expression had replied, "The insurance will pay for it."

That was so unlike Ralph. She had expected him to fly through the roof.

What time did he come to bed? She didn't even know. He was still asleep.

She caught herself fantasizing how it might be if Jay took her and Randy away from all this.

Wow! That was a surprsise.

Certainly she still felt attracted to Jay. It would be fun to live in Los Angeles, lying around a swimming pool, becoming friends with movie stars. Hollywood couldn't be as mundane as he had pictured it the other night.

No way! Even if Jay invited her to come along with him, which he wouldn't, Randy loved his father too much. She couldn't separate the two, even if she was miserable herself. *Damn!* Why couldn't Ralph even try to adjust? Other veterans had lost limbs. Maybe she should push the marriage counselor idea again.

It had been so long since she and Ralph had made love. Perhaps if she, one morning before he started drinking, just took hold of him and tried to make him happy, he might soften; acquiesce to her requests. But, then, could she handle another of his stinging rejections?

So, with all her own problems, why was she sticking her neck out to help Jay?

She tried to marshal her thoughts in that direction. There was no definite answer. It relieved the boredom of Mineral Lake, true, but she supposed it was also a matter of humanity. Could she live with herself if she didn't help? Hopefully, if their positions were reversed, Jay would do the same for her.

Carol rinsed out her mug, then walked to the bedroom to check on Ralph. She didn't have to open the door. His snoring told her he was still out.

Time to go. She glanced at the hallway mirror. Jeans and blouse always looked nice on her; gave her a youthful appearance. What did Helen, Jay's ex, like to wear, she idly wondered.

Retrieving her bag from the living room couch, she headed out the door and to her station wagon. Jay's Skylark was gone. He must be out having a late breakfast.

The ploy had come to her suddenly this morning while she was in the shower. She would tell Maggie she'd envisioned a plan by which they could save each other money, if they joined forces. Maggie, always out to save a buck, would jump at her idea. And, once that happened, getting a cursory tour of the hotel wouldn't be too difficult.

Carol's problem was reaching that point. First, she had to beg the old bitch's forgiveness. That's the part that made her sick.

The lobby of the Murphy Hotel was a potpourri of contradictions. Two huge Remington prints, Indians attacking buffalo, cowboys around a campfire, adorned the walls, covering beige paper bearing faded sketches of small birds in flight. Below the large ceiling fan, which had long since

126

ceased to work, an oversized brown ottoman served as the room's nucleus. This worn circular centerpiece was surrounded by several sofas, chairs, tables and lamps of varying styles, French Provincial, Early American and Spanish. All upholstered pieces were enshrouded with plastic slip covers.

The meticulously-crafted front desk, made of dark cherry wood that badly needed refinishing, was all that remained of the hotel's original 1917 decor, last redone in 1949. It stood in the corner next to stairs that led to the second floor. A box with slots for keys and mail was built into the base of the steps. Sean Murphy, dressed in his white shirt and tie, sat on a high stool behind the desk, engrossed in a copy of *Redbook*.

Directly opposite the main entrance was a long, dimly-lit hallway with guest rooms on either side. At the end of this corridor, a door led outside to a refuse area. This rear exit also gave access to the back part of the children's play yard.

Pausing briefly at the front entrance, Carol pondered as to which room might be David's prison.

Maggie was sitting in her usual spot, next to the picture window that faced Main. The window was draped in such a way as to give her a perfect view of the bank across the street, yet keep her hidden from any passerby. Fat legs spread apart, the widow occupied a squeaky, overstuffed rocker, holding court. Her back-and-forth movement billowed a slight breeze up her tent that helped cool her blubber.

A middle-aged man and woman sat on the sofa opposite Maggie. Carol knew them only as "Miss Johnson," a spinster who always sought the ex-mayor's counsel, and "Shorty," a retired farm worker and fixture at various local taverns. Both were permanent residents of the hotel.

"Nixon will never resign," Maggie was saying. "He's too smart a politician to let a few screaming congressmen force him out."

Shorty scratched at his bushy white mustache, then pushed the dirty Stetson back off his forehead to reveal his balding pate. "I dunno, Maggie. I heard on the radio it could happen any time now."

Miss Johnson, with her gaunt features and thinning white hair, had no comment. She rarely did.

"My goodness," Maggie continued, "I remember back when Harry Truman was in office, there was talk...." She spotted Carol standing by the ottoman. "Well, what brings you here Mrs. Chaney?"

Carol attempted a friendly smile. It wasn't easy. "I was hoping I could speak with you for a few minutes."

"I didn't think we had anything further to say to each other after the other night." The woman maintained her harsh expression; her suspicious, penetrating stare making it difficult for Carol to look directly at her.

"Could we talk privately?"

"I got some things to 'tend to," Shorty said. He gave Carol a cordial glance as he walked by her.

Miss Johnson scowled after him. She knew she'd have to follow his lead, and she'd wanted to stay and sit in on what promised to be an interesting exchange.

After the pair had departed, Carol moved over to the sofa where they'd been roosting. Maggie's eyes offered no invitation to sit, but she did anyway. The old woman's features remained frozen.

"I want to apologize for what happened the other night," Carol began. "We'd had a few drinks before we came to the restaurant and, I guess I got out of line."

No comment from Maggie. Carol mentally cursed her. The old bitch wasn't going to be at all gracious.

"I know how you've tried to help me since I took over Gramps' place. You've given me some very good suggestions. I'm sorry if I've seemed ungrateful."

Still the face remained immobile.

"You know, I've had a lot of personal problems these past few years, with my husband and all...." Carol, figuring a sob or two might work well here, pulled a tissue from her bag to wipe away her few crocodile tears that mixed with perspiration from the room's closeness.

The act worked. Maggie's attitude became motherly. She leaned forward and patted the girl's knee. "Now, now, my dear," she said, "let's have none of that. We all can make mistakes."

Carol milked it. Her sobs grew louder. Sean Murphy glanced up from his magazine to see what was going on.

"My dear," Maggie continued, "the whole incident is forgotten. Don't let it bother you anymore."

"I appreciate that, so very much," Carol said, wiping her nose and giving Maggie what appeared to be a sincere look of gratitude.

The former mayor waited until the girl had regained her composure, then settled back in her chair, assuming her pontifical air again. "Of course, you must be careful of the people you associate with."

Carol thought, "Oh, shit, here comes the lecture."

"Those Barnetts are not well regarded in our town," said Maggie. "Mineral Lake is suffering today because of their selfishness."

"But Jay was only a childhood friend...."

"A Barnett is a Barnett. All those Jews are alike. Don't you know that, child? All they're interested in is money. Lots of money. The Barnetts and people like them should be driven out of our town."

"Jay will be gone for good after Monday. He's only here to sell some real estate."

"Which his father stole!" Maggie acknowledged her visitor's look of surprise. "That's right. Harry Barnett swindled his way into Mineral Lake."

"I... I never...."

"Of course you didn't know. Few people do. Barnett was already well entrenched here before Sam Jackson and a lot of others moved into this town.

"You see, my critics claim that I tried to stop progress here because I wanted to stay the 'queen bee,' so to speak. Well, to be honest, I enjoy the respect I've earned. I won't deny that. But, that's not why I went up against that damn Jew."

Carol was morbidly fascinated by this version of history she'd never heard before. "I don't understand. What did he do?"

"Back in about 1940 or so, I was having some financial problems, paying off medical bills my late husband had run up before he died. The bank already held mortgages on my hotel, my storefronts, and rental houses, so Mr. Barnett offered to loan me the money. It wasn't a benevolent gesture. He took a note on most of my undeveloped land as collateral."

"You mean that all the property the Barnetts used to own here was once yours?"

"Every bit of it!" she spat with a vengeance. "He loaned me less than a fifth of what it was worth. Then, when I fell behind in my payments for one month...thirty days...he invoked an acceleration clause that was in the contract. I had to come up with the entire principal within ten days, or he would take my property."

"And he foreclosed?"

"He took everything. Ten years later, he tried to bring in his other rich Jew friends and turn my land into his own personal gold mine. Well, I was mayor then and I stopped him. What did he do for revenge? He closed down the beach. That's why our town is in the shape it's in."

Carol knew that Maggie was stretching the truth in spots, but she wasn't going to challenge her just now. "I don't think Jay's aware of how his father got your property," she suggested. "He wasn't even born in 1940."

Maggie was adamant. "Like father, like son. One has to pay for the other's sins."

Carol, knowing there was no way to argue against that attitude, shut her eyes momentarily and took a deep breath. It was time to get her plan working. "There's something else I want to speak to you about," she said, trying to keep her voice even.

Maggie seemed receptive to a change of subject.

"Last week," Carol continued, "a man from Alhambra Hotel Supply, that's a new outfit in Spokane, called me. They're trying to establish a clientele in smaller towns like Mineral Lake, and they're offering a pretty good deal. At least, I think it is."

"What's that, my dear?"

"How would you feel about using sheets with patterns in your hotel, rather than white ones?"

"I already use patterned sheets. Is this salesman offering a discount?"

"If we buy ten cases of patterns he has in stock, he'll give us twenty percent off."

"That's a good ten percent better than the service I use now offers. But, ten cases? That's a hundred dozen."

"I thought if we could get several motel owners to go in on this, it wouldn't be such a bad deal. Maybe we could get away with taking one or two cases each. The salesman said we could mix the patterns."

The old woman contemplated the idea. "I'll go for a case or two," she said finally. "Can they match the pattern I have?"

Carol couldn't help but smile. Maggie had just left herself open for the key question. "I'm not sure," she replied cautiously. "I'm planning to drive over to Spokane next week to handle this and some other things. Let me see the patterns you're using, and I'll do my best to duplicate them."

Maggie stared at the girl. Was there a hint of suspicion creeping back behind those eyes? Carol couldn't be sure.

"Why don't you have Sean show me a couple of your empty rooms?" she suggested. "I could get an idea of your color schemes in case we have to make substitutions."

"All the rooms are a brownish yellow," Maggie said slowly. Her steady, probing gaze made Carol uncomfortable. "Sean!"

Sean put his magazine aside and scurried over to his mother. Carol wondered why he always refused to look in her direction.

"Take Mrs. Chaney upstairs and show her the linen closet," Maggie said. "She wants to see our sheet patterns."

Carol didn't know whether Maggie believed her story or not, but since she was getting the short tour, she didn't really care.

As the girl trailed along behind the dutiful Sean, she couldn't help but ponder why they were going upstairs when there was another linen closet on the ground floor, only ten feet away.

TWELVE

Jay parked the Skylark in the alley behind the Murphy Hotel's play yard and shut off the engine. He didn't like being there in the Buick. Even in the dark, Raspy Voice or one of his cohorts might spot him. But, under the circumstances, he had little choice.

He checked his watch. 10:45.

Earlier this evening, Ralph Chaney had announced to Carol that he was going out and taking the station wagon. "You'd damn well better be here when I get back," he'd snarled at her as he'd driven off.

"When he's in that kind of mood," she'd told Jay later in his cabin, "I know not to cross him."

"But, I need you tonight," Jay'd argued.

"I got no other car," she said, "so what difference will it make who drives the Skylark down to Maggie's?...Take the back streets. You're less likely to be seen."

She'd sketched out a rough floor plan of the hotel, marking an "X" by the downstairs linen closet and also the door leading to the cellar. "They wouldn't've hid David in one of the guest rooms," she said. "The walls are paper thin. If he made a noise, somebody would hear him."

"Any suggestions?"

Carol handed him a flashlight. "At the Murphy, they roll up the carpets after ten-thirty. People go to bed early there."

"Even on Saturday night?"

"What's there to do here at night? There's no movies. No bowling...."

"You could watch the grass grow," Jay said with a shrug.

Carol didn't smile. "If you go in through the hotel's back door," she continued, "you probably won't run into anybody."

"And, if I do?"

"You're from Hollywood," she'd shrugged. "Bullshit 'em."

Jay carefully shut the car door, then moved quickly, quietly through the darkened play yard to the refuse area behind the hotel. A scrawny black-and-orange tomcat, feasting on a chicken bone next to the garbage cans, screeched and scampered away as he approached. "Wait for me," Jay quipped.

He moved over to the wood door of the hotel; put his ear against it and listened. Nothing. He grasped the knob; began to slowly turn it. Then, he thought he heard....Were those footsteps approaching the door?

He scooted behind the short fence that separated the refuse area from the play yard and ducked down.

The door opened, spilling a wide beam of light from the hallway out into the refuse area. Sean Murphy, a large filled waste basket in his hands, emerged from the hotel. He yawned, as he dumped the contents into one of the garbage cans. Without looking around, he went back inside, closing the door behind him.

Jay decided to play it safe and stay put for ten minutes. He squatted down; leaned against the fence. Over in the play yard, the black-and-orange tom, was sitting on the bottom of the slide, watching him. "Be patient," Jay said to the animal. "I'll be gone in a couple of minutes." He wished that he didn't have to pee.

He thought about Carol and wondered what was going on between her and Ralph. Was he the violent type? Was she in any real danger? Maybe, when this mess was over, he should ask her to come away with him. Certainly, after all she'd done for him, he owed her that much.

He pondered if he could make it with her in a one-to-one relationship? He still had feelings for her and she, obviously, cared about him. But, they came from two different worlds now. He wasn't about to stay in hers, and he questioned whether she could comfortably fit into the Hollywood scene.

He felt something nudge his leg. The black-and-orange tom had ventured forth, and was rubbing up against him. The cat began to purr. "And, hello to you, too," Jay said, stroking behind the animal's ear.

He waited another five minutes, then crept back over to the door and listened. Silence. He turned the knob and peeked inside.

The carpeted hallway leading to the lobby was long, dark and empty, a single overhead light providing the only illumination. The downstairs linen closet that had aroused Carol's suspicions was at the far end, just this side of the lobby. He'd check there first.

Jay shut the outside door behind him and headed down the corridor, passing by the first "X" on Carol's diagram, the cellar door.

He slowed his pace, shifting to the balls of his feet, as he drew closer to the lobby. Nobody was behind the desk. The large room was empty.

He turned back to the linen closet, anxious to glean its contents. Could there be some clue to David's whereabouts in there? Saying a silent "Please, God," he opened the door to reveal: a closet filled with towels and linens.

"Shit," he muttered. "What the hell did she have in mind?" He was about to close the door when he recalled that, in the movies, closets like these are often fronts for secret passages and stairways.

"Why not?" He reached inside the compartment and rapped against the back wall. It was solid. Nothing hidden there.

"What else could it be?" he thought. This wasn't the movies.

Disappointed, he closed the door and moved back down the hallway toward the cellar. The good news was that the door was unlocked. The bad news: it squeaked when he opened it.

Jay froze, waiting to see if anybody had heard the grating sound. Nothing. Borrowed flashlight switched on, he stepped inside the door and shut it behind him.

He was on a narrow landing, his nostrils taking in the musty air. Lank steps with a wood rail on either side led down to what appeared to be a concrete foundation below. Aiming the light beam ahead of him, Jay started to descend, the wood creaking with each step.

At the foot of the stairs, he could see that the search would not have to be as extensive as he had first thought. Virtually a solid wall of cobwebs, looking like something out of a 1930s Dracula movie, stretched from floor to ceiling, blocking access to the left side of the cellar. Obviously, nobody had disturbed them in years. On the right side of the cavernous room, however, the strands appeared to have been recently brushed aside.

Jay methodically moved the beam around basement, not quite sure what he was seeking. Rusted lawn furniture, worn sofas and overstuffed chairs and old mattresses were amassed against a one wall, while old political campaign posters, proclaiming "Re-elect Mayor Maggie" were piled in the middle of the floor. The placards' colors were red, white and blue, underscoring a scowling photograph of Maggie at their center.

He brushed aside some dangling webbing, and walked toward an old steamer trunk that sat in the far corner amid some rolled-up carpets. Reaching it, he immediately saw that the undisturbed dust on top of the case, like the cobwebs on the other side of the cellar, had to be years old. He began to think that this excursion to Murphy's was just another wild goose chase.

He was about to divert his light elsewhere when he spotted something on the floor next to the trunk.

A large can of poster paint. Black.

He knelt down and touched the rim of the lid. It was tacky. Somebody had made use of the contents quite recently.

Like on a yellow Buick Skylark?

"She's too old and fat, and her son's not the type," he muttered, mocking his own words to Sam the other night.

Suddenly, he was shouting. "You miserable old Nazi bitch!" He grabbed the can's handle and headed for the stairs. He wasn't quite sure what he was going to do with the paint. Maybe he'd splash it all over the hotel lobby, or perhaps he'd just pour it over Maggie's head.

Halfway up the stairs, he stopped. "What did this prove?" he thought. Maggie had a bucket of black paint in her basement. That didn't mean she'd kidnapped David. It didn't even mean that she'd defaced the Skylark. If he went to Ed LaGrange with this "evidence," the lawman would laugh in his face and kick him in the ass.

He held up the can and stared at it for a moment. The fury of frustration boiled inside of him. He let it build. "Fuck!" he screamed, suddenly flinging the paint can across the cellar at one of Maggie's standing placards.

The bucket smashed against the rotund woman's image, bursting open. Its contents splattered over the poster and the surrounding area. As the paint ran down the heavy cardboard, it appeared that Maggie was endowed with a long black beard. She even looked a bit Hasidic.

Jay, his face without expression, watched the paint drops hit the concrete. As he mounted the rest of the steps, he wondered what the hell he was going to do next.

"I *thought* I heard something."

Maggie Murphy was standing in the hallway at the cellar door when Jay opened it. She was wearing a heavy blue woolen bathrobe and her perennial scowl. Her breath engulfed him with the stench of cheap bourbon.

Sean, looking smug, was at his mother's side.

"What are you doing in my basement?" she demanded.

"I...." Jay felt himself flush. The memory of the day that Helen had dropped by his office and discovered him on top of a client, the blonde starlet who'd just been signed for a new television series at Universal, flashed through his head.

He was caught. He was guilty. There was not a damn thing he could say in his defense.

"Shall I call the sheriff?" Sean asked his mother.

Maggie ignored him. "I'm waiting for an answer," she said to the intruder.

Jay's mind raced to find an escape route.

"My mother's waiting for an answer," Sean persisted.

"So am I," Jay replied, recalling the old maxim that the best defense was a good offense.

"I beg your pardon?" The old woman appeared momentarily taken aback.

"That can of black paint down there..."

Now it was Sean's face that reddened.

Jay continued, "...it looks like the kind that decorated my car the other night."

Maggie avoided his steady gaze. "I... I...." she stammered, "I don't know what you're talking about."

"Don't you?" He turned toward the rear door, but her huge frame blocked his path. "Go ahead," he said to Sean, "call the sheriff."

Sean looked at his mother, totally at a loss as to what he should do. Jay seized the moment to head for the lobby.

"Where are you going?" Maggie barked. Jay didn't answer. He kept walking. "Stop him!," she commanded her son.

As Jay entered the unoccupied lobby, he heard the patter of Sean running up the hallway after him, and Maggie muttering, "Damn Jews ruined this town!"

He headed toward the front exit, figuring he'd make a quick dash around to the back of the building before anybody spotted him.

"You just wait!" Sean grabbed hold of Jay's arm as he stepped out onto the sidewalk. "My mother wants to talk to you."

"I don't want to talk to her," Jay said, pulling away and moving toward the side of the hotel. He tried to keep his face turned from the street, in case Raspy Voice was watching.

Sean maneuvered around him, impeding his headway. "You treat my mother with respect," he shouted.

"Same respect I'd give Eva Braun," Jay answered. He glanced around to see if anybody was about. Maggie glowered from the hotel doorway. Up the block, an spindly elderly couple, out for a late night stroll, was ogling the commotion.

"You bastard!" Sean squealed, tears forming in his eyes.

"Get out of my way!" Jay saw a light switch off in the bank across the street. The front door opened and Mr. Parish, the manager, stepped out, locking the door behind him. He turned and looked toward the hotel.

"No!" With a sudden burst of anger, Sean grabbed Jay and pushed his back up against the hotel's plate glass front window. The action caught Barnett off guard. Over Sean's shoulder, he saw Parish hurrying toward them.

POP!

Jay recognized the sound of a gun being fired. Sean was thrust into him. The force of Murphy's body smashed him back into the window. The plate glass shattered. Jay fell backward into the hotel with Sean, a dazed expression on his face, riding atop him.

Maggie screamed as the two men hit the floor. Jay could feel his shirt and back being ripped in several places. He tried to move, but Sean's body held him to the ground.

Parish stood over them, appearing totally bewildered.

"My boy! My boy!" Maggie sobbed.

Jay wasn't sure if Raspy Voice, or Claude Bates or somebody else had fired that shot. All he knew was that the bullet was meant for him.

THIRTEEN

"This one might need stitches." The young resident with the thin, blond mustache picked up a syringe from the prep table and plunged the short needle into Jay's back.

"Ouch!"

"You're actually very lucky," the resident continued. "A piece of that glass could've lodged in your neck. Punctured an artery."

"Yeah, very lucky," Jay repeated, his tone facetious.

"Luckier than Sean Murphy." Ed LaGrange, wearing jeans and a blue short-sleeved sport shirt, had stepped into the treatment cubicle. "Bullet shattered his collar bone. He's got deep cuts all over his face."

"He'll recover?" Jay asked with scant interest.

"He'll recover." LaGrange yawned. "Sorry, I was in bed when Gene called."

"Any idea who did it?"

"We're not even exactly sure where the shot came from," LaGrange said. "We're just small time cops here in Mineral Lake. We gotta wait 'til the state sends their scientific experts to help us investigate."

"You recovered the bullet?"

LaGrange nodded. "A .45. Lots of .45s in town."

"It had to have come from across the street, maybe from one of the rooftops."

LaGrange yawned again. "Probably, but we'll wait for the pros to tell us that."

The last two hours had been a surrealistic nightmare for Jay. He didn't know how long he'd lay on the bed of broken glass with Murphy on top of him; the shards cutting into his flesh.

Maggie was wailing. Other people, nameless faces, were shouting words he didn't really hear. At one point, he remembered that Mr. Parish had bent down and asked if he was okay.

An emergency siren approached, then another one. Somebody finally rolled Murphy off of him. As he felt himself being lifted onto a stretcher, he caught sight of that deputy. What was his name? Gene. The one who'd come when his car had been defaced. He was helping the ambulance driver hoist Murphy's stretcher into the back of the vehicle. Again, Jay wondered if he'd ever met this Gene before.

With Barnett lying on his side, the ride to Mason Hospital had taken less than five minutes. The ambulance attendant spent the entire time working on Murphy, monitoring a needle drip into his forearm. Sean never stopped moaning.

"Can't you give me something?" Jay had asked the attendant, a Hispanic in his mid-thirties. "To help with the pain in my back."

"Doctor has to do that," the man said without looking at him.

Murphy had been rushed into the emergency room first. When Jay's gurney was wheeled in several minutes later, the critically injured man was nowhere to be seen, though Maggie's voice could be heard bellowing orders somewhere in the building.

Jay lay alone in his treatment cubicle for almost fifteen minutes before a black, overweight nurse in her fifties, the kind that seemed to know more about doctoring than most doctors, had stopped in, taken his temperature and blood pressure, given his back a cursory look and announced, "You'll live."

Another half-hour had passed before the young doctor with the blond mustache had arrived and begun digging the shards out of his back.

"Any idea who tried to kill you?" LaGrange asked, as the doctor bandaged Jay's back.

"What makes you think he was trying to kill *me*?" Jay answered without looking at the lawman. "Murphy was the one who got shot."

"If any one wanted to shoot Sean Murphy, they could've done it seven days a week, twenty-four hours a day, for the past several years. You're the new boy in town, and a very unpopular one at that."

"Really?" Jay said, deciding to play dumb.

LaGrange chuckled. "Maggie's talkin' about lynchin' you."

"Me!?!"

"Says none of this would've happened if you hadn't come to town."

"She also tell you that her son was the one who painted on my car the other night?"

"How do you know that?"

Jay started answer, then changed his mind. "Forget it," he said.

LaGrange studied the younger man. "There's something you're not telling me," he said.

"Like what?"

"Like what the hell's goin' on here."

"I'm going to give you something for any residual pain," the resident said, scribbling out a prescription.

"Thanks," Jay said.

"You want a ride?" LaGrange offered.

"My car's down by the hotel."

LaGrange maneuvered his dust-covered Ford station wagon out of the hospital parking lot, heading downtown.

"You must think I'm a smuck," he said to Jay, sitting beside him.

"What?" Jay answered, not sure he'd heard him right.

"A smuck," LaGrange repeated. "You think I'm a smuck."

Jay tried to hide his smile. "It's 'shmuck,' Ed. The word is 'shmuck.'"

"That's what I said. *Smuck!*"

"You're leaving out the 'H,'" Jay chuckled. "It's sh-muck!"

LaGrange didn't smile. "*Smuck!*" he barked. "You know what I mean. You must think I'm a dummy."

"Don't feel bad, Ed," Jay said. "Lots of gentiles have trouble with that one. And, no, I don't think you're a shmuck or a dummy."

"Then why won't you level with me? I know you're in some kind of trouble. Is the Mafia after you, or something?"

"No," Jay smiled.

"Tell me what's going on here?"

Jay flirted with the temptation. "I don't really know," he said, opting for a half-truth.

"Bull!"

"I *don't.*"

They drove in silence until LaGrange stopped the station wagon in front of the Murphy Hotel and its hastily boarded-up front window. "Considering the close relationship I had with your father," he said, turning to Jay, "I'd hope you'd trust me."

Again, Jay fought temptation, and found that the struggle was becoming more difficult. "I can't," he said, opening the car door. "I really can't."

Before LaGrange could respond, Jay was out of the vehicle and heading for the rear of the hotel and the Skylark. The lawman watched him disappear behind the building, then made a U-turn and headed for home. He figured he'd get a few hours sleep, then, in the morning, he'd call Manny Costello, an acquaintance he had with the Seattle P.D., and ask him to run a check on Mr. Jay Barnett.

The black-and-orange tom was "waiting" atop one of the trash cans, licking its paw. "Exciting night, huh, cat?" Jay said, as he walked through the refuse area and entered the dark play yard.
Click!
He stopped just inside the fence. Something was wrong. That metallic sound didn't belong there.
He squinted; his eyes probing the swings and slide in the play area, then the alley beyond where he'd parked the Skylark.
The shadowy figure rose up from behind the vehicle, its arm extended in Jay's direction. There was some object in his hand.
Jay didn't have to guess what the person was holding. He made a quick dive toward the metal slide.
POP!
A bullet ricocheted off the slide just above his head.
POP!
This slug hit the dirt, barely missing his leg.
On his belly beneath the slide, Jay could only see the ground in front of him. He knew he had to move; to get out of there and run, but his legs were frozen, not responding to his brain that was frantically screaming them orders.
"Do it!" he thought. "NOW!"
He started to raise up. His back came into contact with the underside of the slide. It shifted slightly. The metal piece of recreation equipment was not bolted nor set into the ground.
Across the yard, he could hear the person moving toward him. Slowly. Steadily. Confidently.

"Why was Raspy Voice trying to kill him?" Jay wondered, hugging the ground again. "What would that get him?"

Click!

The automatic was cocked once more, ready to fire.

"Maybe it wasn't Raspy Voice," Jay reasoned. "Maybe it was ol' Claude Bates. This was just the kind of stunt he might pull after last night."

Jay dug his right hand into the ground and grabbed a handful of dirt. Maybe, he thought, he could throw it into the bastard's face before he had a chance pull the trigger again.

His assailant drew closer. A smell of stale beer began to permeate the air. From beneath the slide, Jay could see the guy's feet...*or foot*...now. In place of the other extremity was a rubber-tipped crutch.

"Hey, Barnett," Ralph Chaney said. "You like fuckin' my wife?"

"Oh, shit!" Jay muttered to himself, his fear being replaced by anger. "Just what I needed." Still on his belly, he started to inch backward, planning to get to the opposite side of the slide from Chaney.

"Come on, you cocksucker!," Chaney said. "Stand up and take it like a man." He took another step forward. His crutch was within two feet of the bottom of the slide.

Jay stopped his retreat. He knew what he was going to do. "Just one more step," he whispered to himself, sure that his pursuer did not know his exact whereabouts.

Chaney moved closer to the slide.

Jay sprang forward. He grabbed Chaney's crutch, pulling it out from under his arm. The amputee lost his balance and fell backwards.

POP!

The shot went wild as Chaney was sent sprawling. Jay was immediately on top of him, wrestling the .45 automatic out of his hand.

"Bastard!" Chaney screamed.

Jay recovered the weapon. He scrambled to his feet and pointed it at his attacker.

"Go ahead," Chaney continued, raising up on one elbow. "Waste me!"

"Don't tempt me!" Jay's finger was still sore from the splinter. It hurt to squeeze the trigger.

"Do it!" The expression on Chaney's face was more than desperate. It was mournful.

Jay lowered the automatic. "I don't want to 'waste you," he said, quietly. "And, I haven't been boffing your wife."

"Bullshit!"

"We're good friends. She's been helping me." He glanced about. In an upstairs window in the hotel, a light had snapped on.

"Helping you do what?" Chaney asked, his voice distrustful.

"They came from out back," a male voice called from inside the hotel."

"Let's get out of here," Jay said. He handed Chaney his crutch. "In a couple of minutes, Ed LaGrange and his deputy are going to back here to investigate those shots, and you're in enough trouble already."

"Helping you do *what*?" Chaney insisted.

"I'll tell you when we get out of here," Jay said, not sure that he would keep that promise. He reached his hand out to Chaney. After a moment of cogitation, the amputee took hold, using it to steady himself while rising into a standing position.

As they moved together toward the Skylark, they could hear a siren approaching.

FOURTEEN

"I can't believe you fucking did this!" Carol said to her husband. They were in their kitchen. She stood over him, as he sat at the table and stared silently into a mug of black coffee. Jay leaned against the refrigerator. He had no idea that she was capable of such anger.

"What the hell was in your mind!?!" she continued.

Chaney did not look up. "I thought you were fucking him," he said.

"I could be fucking the goddamn cat. That doesn't give you the right to go out and shoot people."

"I'm sorry," Chaney said, tearing up. "I'm sorry. I'm sorry. I'm sorry. Okay?"

"Sorry doesn't cut it anymore."

Jay grimaced at her merciless tirade. Carol had been ripping into Chaney for the past twenty minutes, ever since he'd driven him back home. She reminded him now of Helen, his ex-wife, and he was beginning to feel sorry for the poor dumb bastard. "You got any beer?" he asked, hoping to divert her attention.

"In the frig," she said, not taking her eyes off of her husband.

"Toss me one," Chaney said to Jay.

"Don't you dare!" Carol barked. She turned back to Chaney. "If you ever drink again, me and Randy are out of here. For good!"

"Ralph," Jay said, opening the refrigerator, "what put it into your head that Carol and I were fooling around?" He grabbed a bottle of Olympia and shut the door. The cold glass soothed his injured hands.

"Got a phone call." Chaney said.

"Who from?" Carol asked.

"A friend."

Jay took a sip of beer. "His name Claude Bates?"

Chaney nodded. "How'd you know?"

"Lucky guess." Jay looked at Carol. "The act of an angry…very stupid man."

"Claude is the one who smashed up the station wagon," Carol said.

"Why would he do that?" Ralph asked.

Jay quickly detailed the events of the previous evening.

"That son-of-a-bitch!" Ralph said.

"That's not important, now." Dejected, Carol plopped down onto a kitchen chair. "The sheriff's going to be here before long to arrest my moron husband; Sean Murphy will sue us for everything we've got...*and get it....*"

"Maybe not." Jay interrupted. "Ralph, where'd you park your station wagon?"

"Couple blocks from the hotel."

"Did anybody see you?"

"No. Don't think so."

"Okay," Jay said. He turned to Carol. "Let's go pick it up and bring it back here."

"What are you thinking?" Carol asked.

"Ed LaGrange is no Sherlock Holmes," Jay explained. "Nobody's been killed. Not even too badly hurt. The State cops aren't going to give this case high priority."

Carol started to object. "Yeah, but...."

"Bring the wagon back here," Jay said, "and there's nothing to tie Ralph to the shooting. All LaGrange has is a .45 slug."

"Why are you doin' this?" Chaney asked warily.

"Your wife is my friend," Jay replied. "Besides, I got more important things on my mind just now."

"Like what?"

"Like my son's been kidnapped," Jay blurted, "and she's trying to help me get him back."

"Kidnapped!?!" Chaney appeared dazed by the sudden revelation. "That little kid?"

"That little kid," Jay repeated. He was surprised that he suddenly felt he could confide in Chaney, yet he did.

"When did this happen?"

"The morning after I got into town."

"Why didn't you call the cops?"

"The kidnappers.... They've got some sort of 'in' with the police."

"I'll call Gene Thomas, LaGrange's deputy." Chaney reached for the telephone. His shift in manner indicated a sincere concern. "We shoot pool together."

"No!" Jay snapped. "I don't trust that guy." He emitted a deep sigh. "I don't know *who* to trust in this town."

Chaney's eyes were steady and sober. "Trust me," he said.

"Trust *you*!?!" Jay tried not to smirk. "Why should I trust you?"

"'Cause I got a kid, too."

Jay glanced at Carol. Her expression had softened. Moisture was in her eyes, as she watched her husband.

"And," Chaney continued, "this is the kind of work I did in 'Nam."

"What kind of work is that?" Jay asked.

"I found people."

"You were an M.P.?"

Chaney shook his head. "Special Forces," he said. "We did 'spook jobs'?"

"Spook Jobs?"

"Yeah, we'd go in at night north of the D.M.Z. and look for downed pilots...before they became P.O.W.s."

"That had to be dangerous work," Jay said, impressed.

"That's how I got this." Chaney patted his artificial leg. "Sniper got me just as we were bein' picked up by our chopper."

"Ralph," Jay said, choosing his words carefully, "I appreciate your wanting to help, but this isn't Viet-Nam. What can you do that we already haven't tried?"

"I was the best," Chaney said, matter-of-factly. "I've got a nose for finding people."

"His buddies called him 'Bloodhound'," Carol said with a renewed pride in her voice. She stroked her husband's cheek.

It surprised Jay that he felt a momentary tinge of jealousy.

"He's got a drawer full of medals and citations, Carol continued."

For the first time since he'd met the man, Jay could see that Chaney was displaying an enthusiasm; a sense of purpose. He still wasn't quite convinced that he should entrust his son's life to this less than stable veteran, yet, watching Carol beam at him, he wasn't about to burst his bubble either. "What do you suggest?" he asked.

"First off," Chaney said, adopting a 'take charge' attitude, "bring me up to date. Tell me everything that's happened since you got to Mineral Lake."

Jay spent the next twenty minutes giving Chaney a step-by-step account of his activities since arriving in the resort town. He wiped away a tear when he described the moment when David had disappeared, then continued the narrative in his matter-of-fact writer's style. Carol listened silently, only occasionally interjecting a detail that he may have omitted.

"We've pretty much ruled out the Storyman and Maggie," Jay concluded. "But this Larry Palmer guy, the reporter, is still an enigma."

"Reconnaissance," Chaney said. "He was probably setting you up for the snatch."

"I'm sure you're right," Jay agreed.

Chaney took another swig of coffee, pondering for a moment. "Tell me about this movie of yours?" he said.

"What does that have to do with anything?"

"Maybe nothing," Chaney said. "Just tell me about it."

"It's called *Repercussions*. It's a relationship movie...budgeted at just under two hundred thousand."

"And you put up all that money yourself?!?"

"All the cash," Jay said. "Went into hock to do that. Most of it, though, is on deferment."

"You mean, everybody works for nothing?"

Jay nodded. "Until I sell the picture. That's how most low budget movies get made."

"And, if you don't sell it?"

"The lab takes the movie," Jay shrugged. "They auction it off for their fees."

"So," said Chaney, "who gains if you lose the movie?"

Jay shook his head. "I see where you're going with this, Ralph, and you're on the wrong track. This isn't *The French Connection*. It isn't *The Godfather*. It's not that kind of movie. It's an art house film.

"I mean, if we're lucky, we get good reviews and I break even. The pay-off would be that some major studio is impressed enough with my work to hire me to write and direct something for them."

Chaney lit a cigarette and took a long drag. "There's one thing that I am sure about," he said, finally. "This kidnapping.... It has nothing to do with ransom. There's something else involved."

"Like what?" Carol asked.

"If we know that, then we'll know who did it, won't we?"

Jay deliberated for a moment, then slowly gave voice to his thoughts. "It's almost as if these people are more interested in keeping me confined than in the ransom," he said.

"Exactly," Chaney agreed, stifling a yawn. "Maybe they're afraid that you might stumble onto something."

Carol repeated her previous question. "Like *what*?"

"Damned if I know," said Chaney. He glanced at the wall clock. "And, at three o'clock in the morning, my brain is too tired to figure it out."

"I didn't realize it was so late," Jay said. "I really appreciate your getting involved."

Chaney shrugged a noncommittal response.

Jay turned to Carol. "Shall we go pick up the station wagon?"

"Let me get my purse."

Her exit from the room was aborted by the shrill ring of the telephone. "Who the hell could that be at this hour?" she asked, reaching for the receiver.

Jay grabbed her hand. "I think it's for me," he said.

"Oh, my God!" Carol said, her face paling. She took an involuntary step backwards, exchanging an anxious glance with her husband.

"I wish we could trace this." Jay said. "He picked up the receiver. "Hello?"

"Daddy?" David's tearful voice seemed distant and frightened.

"Daver?" A fusion of relief and dread passed through Jay. He glanced over at his hosts.

"Jesus!" Chaney muttered. Carol gripped his shoulder.

"Daddy," the child said, "come get me."

"Where are you, Dave?" Jay said, eagerly. "I'll be right there."

"He's with me." The raspy voice sent an immediate chill through Jay. "And, you haven't been following directions."

"You son-of-a-bitch," Jay shouted, "I want my son!"

David, suddenly, screamed in pain.

"Leave him alone!" Jay yelled, his eyes filling with tears.

"Then," the caller said, tauntingly, "play by the rules."

"The rules?" Jay repeated.

"Stop playing detective."

He let David scream once more before he hung up.

FIFTEEN

Jay picked at his breakfast.

He punctured the egg yolk with his fork, then watched the thick yellow liquid pour out and collide with the thin slice of ham on the other side of the plate. Absently, he tore off a piece of toast, used it to wipe up some of the goo and popped it into his mouth. The taste seemed to whet his appetite. He wolfed down the rest of his meal, then leaned back in his booth, shut his eyes and listened to the grating sound of the restaurant's air conditioning wall unit. "Those bushings need oiling," he thought.

He'd hardly slept at all last night. He'd had another nightmare about the phantom and Jerry Roscoe. What did Jerry have to do with all this?

David's frightened screams of pain had kept pounding at him, while his mind raced through a dozen scenarios as to what Raspy Voice was doing to his son.

One thing was certain, when this matter was over, he would kill Raspy Voice.

It made no difference as to whether David was returned in perfect health or not. That son-of-a-bitch was going to die.

"Fuck 'im!" he said, as gulped down the last of his coffee.

"What!?!" The blonde waitress, with two plates of eggs in her hands, had stopped halfway to her table and was glowering at him. So were the half dozen customers in Al's Cafe.

Jay felt his face turn crimson. "Sorry, folks," he said, "I was just thinking aloud."

"You'd better keep them kind of thoughts to yourself, mister," the girl said. "Especially on a Sunday." She turned on her heel and headed for her table.

Jay slid out of the booth, threw a five down onto the table and, without looking directly at anyone, strode out the door.

The heat hit him like a blast oven. Perspiration poured down his forehead, as he unlocked the Skylark. He dreaded another useless day in his cabin.

Turning the key in the ignition, he looked through the windshield. Parked down and across the street were a green Ford pick-up with a battered left fender, a current model beige Dodge Coronet and a blue Chevy van. "Sure ain't Beverly Hills," he mused without smiling.

He made a U-turn, and headed in the direction of the Franklin Trailer Court. He wondered what, if anything, Ralph Chaney was doing this morning. He'd certainly been impressed by the man's sudden take-charge attitude last night, but perhaps that was all talk. Things always looked different; more realistic in the light of morning. What could Chaney do that he hadn't already tried?

As he drove past the Presbyterian Church that stood atop the hill overlooking the business district, Jay saw that Sunday morning services were about to begin. He recognized the sour-pussed, matronly teller from the bank entering the wood-framed structure. She was accompanied by a portly, gray-haired man of her approximate age, who Jay took to be her husband.

He glanced in his rearview mirror and noticed that the blue Chevy van that had been parked by Al's Cafe was now following about a half block behind him. He turned his attention back at the road ahead.

Suddenly, he recalled that he'd been seeing quite a few blue Chevy vans since he'd arrived in Mineral Lake.

"Are there a lot of them in this town," he thought, "or is that the same one?"

Jay struggled to remember where and when he'd seen the vans. Yes, it was in front of the bank, and he had seen a blue van there just before David was taken. Excited with the prospect that he might finally be onto something concrete, Jay decided to try an experiment.

He hung a left one block before the Franklin Trailer Court, figuring that he'd circle the block and see if the Chevy followed him.

The van did not make the turn. "Shit!" Jay muttered, his eye locked on the rearview mirror. He continued around the tree-lined residential block.

He'd just made the right turn that brought him in front of the Franklin Court driveway, when he glanced again into the mirror. The blue van was parked at the curb, one block further west from the court entrance. "Holy shit!" he beamed. "Clever, clever, clever."

Jay waited for a VW bug to pass by, then made a quick U-turn, intending to catch up with the Chevy and confront the driver, but as he straightened out the Skylark, he saw that the van was no longer in sight.

"What the hell!?!" He pressed down on the gas and sped up to the spot where he'd seen the vehicle parked. There was no sign that it had ever been there.

He turned left at the next corner. proceeding slowly up the street, checking every driveway for the elusive van. He saw a beat-up red Falcon, a gray Dart, and even a beige van bearing the sign, "Mineral Lake Plumbing". No blue Chevy. "Where the fuck did you go?" Jay asked aloud.

He briefly considered backtracking; knocking on the door of each and every house on this tree-lined street, and asking the resident if they knew somebody on their block who owned such a vehicle. Instead, he turned right at the next corner, and continued his search down the next parallel street with similar results.

The next street over was not as well kept as the first two. Devoid of many trees, virtually all of the homes were fronted with bleached lawns, long dead from the Sun's harsh rays. After no luck spotting the van on this barren road, Jay began to wonder if he'd been imagining the vehicle altogether.

Thirty minutes later, Jay pulled into the Franklin Court and parked in front of the office. "Who in town has a blue Chevy van?" he asked Chaney, who greeted him at the screen door.

"Blue Chevy van?" Chaney started to speak, then hesitated. He thought for a moment, then shrugged. "Lots of people, I guess" he said. "Why?"

"Because one's been following me, and I think it might belong to the kidnapper."

Chaney responded with a non-committal, "Huh."

At the kitchen table, Jay ardently recounted the morning's events to Carol and Ralph. "I only wish I'd gotten a look at the driver," he concluded.

"I don't know who drives a blue van," Carol said, turning to her husband. "Do you?"

Chaney shook his head. "Not off-hand," he said. "It makes sense, though. If you want to grab a kid fast, a van's the right vehicle to do it with."

Jay suddenly paled, his fervor turning to apprehension. "I think I fucked up," he announced, standing up.

"What?" Carol asked.

"If that was the guy, then he knows that I'm on to him. He might...." Jay stopped himself in mid-sentence. He turned away from the couple, choking back a sob, as he stared out the window.

"Jay," Carol said, compassion enfolding her words, "he wouldn't do that."

"Yes, he would." Chaney said.

"Ralph!" Carol admonished her husband.

"Let's not kid around, Carol!" Chaney's tone was compelling. "If this asshole panics, you don't know what he's going to do." He limped over to Jay, and put his hand on his shoulder. "It's time for some bold moves."

"Like what?" Jay asked.

"Like let's get some professional help."

Jay smirked. "Like Ed LaGrange and his dumb deputy?"

"No," Chaney smiled. "More like Sam Jackson."

"Sam?" The idea intrigued Jay.

"You trust him, don't you?

"Sure, but...."

"He's got friends with the State Police." Carol said.

"Fine," Jay said, moodily, "but how am I supposed to get to him without being seen?"

"All arranged," Chaney smiled. "I've made you an appointment."

SIXTEEN

Ralph Chaney had a hunch. If he was right, he'd be the hero of the hour. Hell, he'd be the hero of the century!

He needed to be a hero just now. He needed it to regain his wife's respect. He needed it to restore his own feeling of self-worth.

Last night, in the kitchen with Carol and Barnett, he could sense a change in attitude in both of them. He was asking pointed questions, using his past experience in 'Nam to try to help, and they were looking at him differently. With surprise. With respect.

He was just improvising then. Just wait until he did some serious investigation, and he'd really be hot.

That was the first time in over two years that he'd felt any kind of fondness, regard from his wife. Usually, she just tried to hide her disgust at his drunkenness and self-pity.

Who could blame her? He acted like an asshole most of the time. Brooding. Snapping at her. Pushing her around. And, as far as sex was concerned, what the hell was that? He could hardly even get it up any more.

This was an opportunity to change all of that permanently. Sure, he wanted to get that poor little kid back safely. He wouldn't even mind wasting the goddamn kidnapper himself. Bastards like that *should* be wasted.

But, he wanted to do it. He was going to do it. And, that would get his life back on track again.

He thought about when he'd played basketball, dribbling the ball down the court, weaving in-and-around the opposing players, then with a quick leap, he'd smash the ball down through the hoop. Damn, he missed those golden days.

"That's gone!" he said aloud, forcing himself out of the reverie. "It's over!"

If only he hadn't gotten Carol knocked up…

He hated that job at the supermarket. "Management trainee," *bullshit*! He was nothing more than a glorified cashier and, on a slow day, they'd have him back working as a box boy.

That's why he'd enlisted in the Army.

He was bored at work and even more bored at home. Sure, Carol did her best to make him happy. He guessed he loved her. Randy was cute…when he wasn't bawling. But damn, he was too young back then to be married…to take on the responsibilities of a husband and father.

Compared to his life in Yakima, Vietnam sounded like it would be a patriotic blast.

That was before he got there.

If only the chopper had been a minute or two earlier that night…

If only the moon hadn't been so full…

If only he'd run a little faster…

If only Charlie hadn't been such a good shot…

If only…

And, that's over, too! *What's done is done!*

But, if he could pull this one off. If he could save that little boy… My God! He could write his own ticket.

Hell, he might even open his own private detective agency. Find other kids…*anybody* who was missing. You didn't need two legs for that. You just had to be good at your job.

That's what he'd do! He and Carol would sell the trailer court. They'd move to a big city, Seattle, Spokane, or even Portland maybe…and he'd open up an office.

If only his hunch was right…

He popped a Ritz cracker into his mouth and looked through the kitchen window. Carol was still out there on the lawn, talking with that middle-aged couple from Vancouver, who had just registered. As soon as she walked them back to their cabin, he'd sneak out and be on his way.

The house where he was headed was less than three blocks from there. It would be a brisk walk, even with his prosthesis. He could be there, check out what he wanted, and be back at the court in plenty of time to smuggle Barnett up to Sam Jackson's.

Of course, if he was right, there wouldn't be any need to see Sam Jackson at all.

He limped back to the bedroom and retrieved his .45 from the dresser drawer where Carol had temporarily hidden it last night. "First chance I get tomorrow," she'd said, "I'm throwing the damn thing into the lake."

He didn't dare argue with her.

Chaney figured he could have the weapon back in the drawer before she missed it, but he wasn't about to stroll up to that house without protection. He checked the clip. There were still four rounds in it. He shoved the piece into his belt, adjusted his faded Hawaiian shirt so that the bulge didn't show and trekked back to the kitchen.

Carol and the Canadians were nowhere in sight. Within seconds, he was through the door and hobbling out the front entrance of the trailer court.

He headed west on Main. If he remembered correctly, the house was located two blocks over on Maple Avenue.

His memory had been triggered when Barnett had mentioned the blue Chevy van that had "disappeared" two blocks away. He was sure he knew the driver of that vehicle. He knew his house. And, if driver and kidnapper were one and the same, all hell was going to break loose in Mineral Lake.

"It'll be a hot time in the old town tonight," he said to himself, as he crossed Oak Street. Ignited, he quickened his pace, even though the prosthesis was beginning to cause him some discomfort.

He began to toy with a plan of action. He had thought of knocking on the door and announcing that he was walking by and just stopped in to say, "hello," but his military training caused him to veto that immediately.

Reconnaissance was what Special Forces had taught him. Before approaching a potential enemy, you check out the territory; see what you're up against.

"Hello, Mr. Chaney." Seventy-year-old Mrs. Briar was hosing down her flower bed, as he turned north onto Maple.

Ralph nodded to the gaunt woman in the yellow print sun dress and wide-brimmed straw hat. He did not want to get into a gab fest with her.

"How were those apricot preserves?" she asked.

"Delicious," he said, not stopping. "Thanks again."

"I'll bring you some more."

"Great!" He continued up the street.

"How's Mrs. Chaney?" she called.

He didn't look back. "Fine."

He spotted the house, a single-story clapboard box with an asphalt roof, built during the 1920s. The beige paint had started peeling long ago, and what had once been a lawn had evolved into a blanket of dandelions and other wild flowers.

Nobody appeared to be around. He walked up the dirt driveway that ran along the side of the structure until he reached the weed-filled turnaround area in the rear. There was no garage in the yard, which was enclosed by a weather-beaten six-foot olive green picket fence. No blue van. The only vehicle present was a rusted bicycle, minus wheels, leaning against the wall next to a pile of discarded automobile tires.

Chaney began to wonder if he'd made a mistake. He was sure this was the right house. Or, was it?

He'd only been here twice before. Both times at night. And, those times, he'd been drinking.

He mounted the five wooden steps to the back porch and knocked on the door. No answer. He knocked again, harder. Still no response.

Discouraged, Chaney started back down the steps, then changed his mind. "What the fuck," he said to himself. "I came all the way over here. What's a little breaking and entering?"

He grasped the door handle and turned it. He was surprised when the door swung open. "Hello!" he called inside. "Anybody home?" Again, no answer. "Company's here," he shouted. Silence.

He glanced around to make sure that nobody was watching, then stepped inside the house and shut the door behind him.

The kitchen was familiar. He'd definitely been there before, playing poker at the plastic and metal table in the center of the room. There'd been dirty jokes, laughter and plenty of beer spilled that night. Claude Bates had been there...others....

The room then had been a mess with beer bottles, nudie magazines, chips and dip strewn about. Today, the place was immaculate. The counter tops were wiped clean. Dishes and glasses were put away. Everything was in its proper place.

"Didn't know he was such a good housekeeper," Chaney mused. He started down the short dim hallway that led to the front of the house. The passageway's only illumination was from the narrow shard of sunlight that filtered around the drawn window shade on the front door.

Chaney glanced into the living room. The room did not look lived in. Its upholstered and wooden furniture was well chosen, but old. In all likelihood, a woman had selected the French Provincial pieces well over twenty years ago.

A portable television was in the master bedroom, facing an unmade queen-sized bed. Indeed, the mess that Chaney remembered from the kitchen poker game seemed to have been transferred intact into this room. Empty beer bottles, girlie magazines and crumb-filled pizza boxes sat on the dresser, covered most of the bed and much of the floor. "This is more like it," Chaney chuckled to himself.

He heard a light thumping, a double thumping. The sound seemed to emanate from the house's second bedroom across the hall.

Outside, he heard an automobile pass by. Or, did it stop?

Chaney's first instinct was to get the hell out of there. He was, after all, an intruder. Another thump. He patted the .45 under his shirt for assurance, then stepped to the bedroom door and turned the handle.

Like the kitchen hallway, the room was dimly lit by the small amount of sunlight that escaped through the drawn window shade. It was sparsely furnished with a dresser, a small whirring electric fan atop it, and a single twin-sized bed. Only a large poster of James Dean in *Rebel Without a Cause* decorated the wall. The stench of urine and feces permeated the room.

The young boy lay on the bed, blindfolded, gagged, his hands cuffed behind his back; his feet bound and tied with a chain to the bed's leg.

"Oh, Jesus!" Chaney said, recognizing the child as Barnett's son. "Jesus fucking Christ!" He hobbled over and sat on the bed.

"It's going to be okay, son," he said, as he attempted to remove the cloth from the child's mouth. "I'm here to help you."

David coughed repeatedly, as the gag was removed, and Chaney began working on the hand towel that covered his eyes. "Where's my daddy?" the child sobbed, terrified. "I want my daddy."

"I'm going to take you to your daddy, son," Chaney assured him. "Just as soon as I get you untied."

His blindfold removed, David stared at Chaney, frightened, not quite sure how to react. "Are you a policeman?" he asked.

"I'm Ralph," Chaney said, forcing a smile. "You and your daddy are staying at my trailer court."

"With Carol?" David's eyes appeared tentatively hopeful.

Chaney nodded. "She's my wife," he said, his smile becoming more genuine.

David began to calm. The corners of his mouth started an upward movement. His gaze wandered to the bedroom door. Suddenly, a renewed expression of horror brushed across his face.

"What is it, son?" Chaney asked.

Before the boy could answer, something sharp punched Chaney in the back. His breathing became stifled. He looked down at his shirt. It was drenched with blood. His blood. The tip of what looked to be a long knife protruded from his chest.

The final image recorded in his brain was David starting to open his mouth, as if he were going to scream.

SEVENTEEN

Carol Chaney was fuming as she knocked on the screen door of Jay's cabin.

"Come on in," he called. The door to the bathroom was ajar.

"I don't know where the hell he is," she said, "but this is just like him." She shut the screen door and plopped down on the chair opposite Jay's bed.

"Where's *who*?"

"My husband! That's who!"

"He's not here?"

"That's what I've been trying to tell you."

"He could be out running an errand," Jay said, entering from the bathroom. He was drying his face with a hand towel.

"He *could* be out tying one on."

"Come on," Jay said, buttoning his shirt. "He was just fine a couple of hours ago."

"I'm married to him," she retorted. "I've seen him 'just fine' hundreds of times, then he decides that one drink will help him to think better."

She glanced around the room. "How do you stand it in here? It's so hot."

"It's the perfect sauna," he quipped. "I figure I've shed twenty pounds since yesterday."

She didn't smile.

Jay looked at his watch. "It's almost time to head to Sam's."

"I know." She stood up and muttered, "Where the hell are you, Ralph?"

"Maybe this isn't a good idea after all?" Jay said, hesitantly. "I mean, going to see Sam?"

"Why?"

"It's broad daylight. The kidnapper might spot me."

"And, the sky might fall. You gotta take a chance."

"I've *been* taking chances, he said, "and they've all backfired. I'm just afraid of making another wrong move."

"You can trust Sam."

"I know I can," he said.

"Besides, whoever this asshole is, he won't be expecting you to sneak around during the day, will he?"

"Probably not," Jay had to agree. "You'll drive me?"

"Who else?" she shrugged. "I've got to come right back, though. It's Sunday, and we've got a couple of reservations due in this afternoon."

"That's good."

"Somebody's got to be here to watch the store."

"I'll get Sam to bring me home," Jay said.

"Home!" she repeated, half to herself; her tone bitter. "This is no *home*."

"Spunky," Jay said, "don't convict the poor guy before you find out what's going on."

"I told you. I know what's going on."

Wiping her eye with the back of her hand, she stood up and opened the screen door. "I'll get the car," she said as she walked outside.

Jay wondered if he should've gone to her, given her a comforting hug. He wished that he had. "Shit!" he muttered, letting his true feelings emerge.

Chaney was all talk. Jay suspected that Carol was probably right about that. He was out now getting plastered.

"You fucking bastard!" he said. "You build up my hopes...." Suddenly, he was shouting. "It's not *your* son that's missing!"

He knew he was stupid to have counted on somebody else to carry the ball for him. Nobody ever had before. Despite any help he was getting from Carol or would get from Sam, he was in this thing alone. In the final analysis, David's life depended on him.

Carol pulled the Dodge wagon up to the cabin door and motioned to Jay. "Coast is clear," she said.

As he'd done the other night, he slipped out of the cabin and into the vehicle's back seat. He tried to make himself comfortable on the floor.

"No blue Chevy vans in sight," Carol said, as she turned out of the driveway and headed the Dodge toward the town's business area.

"Forget the van," Jay said, raising himself up on one elbow. "If he knows I made him today, he'll switch cars."

"Okay," Carol quipped. "I'll look for a red van."

"With polka-dots," Jay added.

"And, happy faces," she smiled.

They drove in silence for a block. "What do you hear about the shooting last night?" Jay asked.

"That's all they were talking about at the market," she said. "Millie, the check-out lady, thinks that *you* did it."

"Me!?!" Jay couldn't help but smile. "How could I have done it?"

Carol chuckled. "I asked 'er. She said, 'I don't know for sure. But, them Barnetts are bad people. They got the money to do anything.'"

"Maggie still planning to send a lynch mob after me."

"There's talk of it."

"What!?!"

"Just kidding." Carol laughed.

"Nothing would surprise me in this town," Jay said. "How's Sean?"

"They say he'll go home in a couple of days, but I understand that Maggie's still pretty hysterical. I think the doctors gave her some sort of tranquilizer."

They drove past the Murphy Hotel where two young boys were adorning the boarded-up front window with graffiti. At the corner, Carol turned, then headed down the alley of the next block.

"Ralph told me that Sam's leaving his back door unlocked," she said, slowing as they approached the print shop. "I'll stop in front of it. You can jump out, and...."

She stepped on the brakes.

"What's the matter?" Jay asked, wondering why she'd stopped talking mid-sentence.

"I don't believe this," she said.

"What?"

"Take a look."

Jay poked his head up and looked out the window. "Oh, shit!" he said, feeling himself blanch.

Parked next to Sam Jackson's print shop was a blue Chevy van.

EIGHTEEN

Ed LaGrange hung up the phone, then reached for the coffee mug on his desk. The liquid had turned lukewarm, but he still downed it in one gulp. He leaned back in his chair, and studied the various state and federal "Wanted" posters that hung haphazardly on his walls; portraits of criminals who would never come anywhere near Mineral Lake.

His phone conversation with Sgt. Manny Costello of the Seattle Police Department had been both enlightening and disturbing. He didn't quite know what to make of the information.

Even though it was Sunday, Costello had done LaGrange a favor and run a quick check on Jay Barnett with the cops down in Los Angeles. The eldest son of Harry Barnett had no criminal record himself, however, as a Hollywood publicist, the police were well aware of him and his efforts to get his various clients out of trouble when they'd crossed over the legal limits.

"You know that television actor?" Costello had asked. "The one who plays a private eye with a black patch on his eye?"

"I don't watch much TV," LaGrange admitted.

"You should. That's a good show."

"What's your point?"

"The guy got drunk one night. Smashed up a fancy restaurant on the Sunset Strip. Then, your boy, Barnett, showed up, promised that his client would pay all damages, and that pretty much kept the incident out of the papers."

"Wasn't anybody arrested?"

"I told you. Those cops down there like your boy. He's very generous around Christmas time."

LaGrange pondered a moment. "Anything else?" he asked.

"He's currently on his ass." Costello said.

"What do you mean?"

"He's broke. Hocked everything he has and then some."

"How's that?"

"He decided he wanted to be a movie director. The problem is he ignored the first rule of successful movie-making?"

"Which is?"

"He put up his own dough. Now, if he doesn't pay off his creditors pretty damn quick, he's going to lose the whole ball of wax."

"Jesus," LaGrange said, thinking out loud, "maybe he's up here selling off the rest of his family's property."

"That info help you out?" Costello had asked.

"Yeah," LaGrange said, terminating the call. "Thanks, Manny."

Tapping his pencil against the empty coffee mug, LaGrange wondered, if all Barnett was doing in Mineral Lake was disposing of his real estate holdings, why was he being so secretive about it?

What was he doing with Sean Murphy?

And, most importantly, who was shooting at him and for what reason?

"I'm leaving, now, Edwin," Sarah Dooley said from the doorway, checking the contents of the large carpetbag that she always carried with her.

Broad-shouldered and six-feet tall, the sixty-seven-year-old Sarah worked mornings as City Clerk and afternoons, across town, as Mineral Lake's librarian. Her Clerk facility was next to LaGrange's office/one-cell jail in the City Hall, a single-story building that also housed the truck and equipment of the community's volunteer fire department.

LaGrange didn't mind so much that this often brusque matron was a crony of Maggie Murphy's, or that she usually wore the ugliest print dresses that he'd ever seen. He just didn't like the way she spoke to him, and just about every other male. She was like a school teacher talking to a bunch of ten-years-olds.

"See you tomorrow," he said.

"Tuesday," she corrected. "Clerk's office will be closed tomorrow. I have to take Earl to Spokane for his dialysis treatment."

"How is Earl?" he asked, referring to her husband.

"Home watching his baseball game on the television."

"And, you're off to the library?"

"Where else would I be going?"

"It's Sunday." LaGrange shrugged. "You should take a day off?"

"Mayor Kanaly's on vacation. I've got twice as much work to do."

"What's so pressing at the library?" LaGrange asked, concealing his amusement at her over-dedication.

"Mr. Mazolla donated a box of old books last week, and they have to be catalogued."

"Anything interesting?"

"I think there's a couple Agatha Christie's."

He shook his head. "I like Mickey Spillane."

"That's your problem, Edwin" Sarah responded. "You've never been exposed to good literature."

"That's not true," LaGrange said, a mischievous gleam in his eye. "I read all of my kid's *Classics Illustrated*.

"Very funny." She did not smile, simply turned on her heel and departed.

The lawman chuckled to himself, as he walked across the room to refill his coffee mug from the percolator next to the room's sole window. His first sip was interrupted by the voice of his deputy.

"Sheriff!"

LaGrange strolled over to his desk and grabbed the microphone to the short wave radio. "What is it, Gene?" he asked.

"I'm out on Darby Road."

"What the hell you doin' out there?"

"Patrolin'."

"You're paid to patrol in town, Gene," LaGrange said, thinking that the deputy was out visiting his girlfriend, Evie Randall, on city time. "Farmlands are *county* territory."

"I know that, Sheriff," Gene replied, "but I got a dead man here."

"A dead man!?!"

"Yeah, it's Ralph Chaney. Somebody killed 'im."

"What!?!" LaGrange said, trying to fathom the news. "Who's dead?"

"Ralph Chaney."

"Jesus Christ!" LaGrange said, grabbing his hat. "I'll be right there."

As he hurried to his police car behind the City Hall, LaGrange couldn't help speculating what Jay Barnett might have to do with all this.

NINETEEN

"Sure, that's my Chevy van out back," Sam Jackson said, not dismounting the three-foot stool upon which he sat. "If it didn't need a valve job, I'd be using it for pick-ups and deliveries." He grabbed a capital "Y" from the block letter boxes on his work bench and placed it into the type he was setting.

"Jesus," he continued, "I got more important things to do than follow you around all day."

"I'm sorry, Sam," Jay said. "I'm very paranoid over this. I'm beginning to suspect everybody."

"Next, you'll say that was me shooting at you last night outside the Murphy Hotel."

"Don't be silly."

"Any idea who the culprit was?"

"No," Jay replied, throwing a glance at Carol, who had remained standing by the back door ever since they'd sneaked through it.

"Hey, if my kid had been snatched," Sam said, "I'd be paranoid, too. I'd be running around here like a goddamn lunatic… Let's just get the little guy back. Okay?"

Jay nodded, trying to hide his emotion.

"Ralph pretty much filled me in," Sam said. "I would've made some calls, but I didn't, because he said to talk to you first. I think we should get the Feds in on this. They're the pros."

Jay looked at Carol. "He's right," she said.

"I'll see you later," Jay said.

"Go ahead, Carol," Sam said. "I'll run this mug home."

She opened her mouth to say something, then decided against it. Shaking her head, she disappeared out the door.

"I'm not sure about calling in the F.B.I.," Jay said. "This guy claims he's got...connections."

"He's bluffing. If he's got you too scared to take a shit, you're going to do what he says."

"I wasn't even going to call you."

"That's what Ralph told me." Sam turned back to his type-setting. "What about Ed LaGrange? He'd help you."

"Absolutely not," Jay said. "He's local."

"He's also a good guy." Sam emitted a short, frustrated chuckle. "You're sure not easy. Kind of like your old man."

"Sorry," Jay said.

"He sure as hell had a mind of his own." Sam deposited three more block letters into his line of type. "I got some ideas," he said, "but just give me a minute here. I got this customer going out of town in the morning, so he wants to come in and proof this flyer today."

"I wondered why you were working on a Sunday," Jay said.

"I always work on Sunday," Jackson replied. "It gives me something to do"

While Jackson finished his type-setting, Jay strolled around the cavernous back room of the print shop. The large press, along with the ancient linotype machine, sat like silent museum pieces on one side of the room, next to a pile of bound volumes that apparently contained every published copy of the *Mineral Lake Bulletin.*

He smiled to himself, recalling the Thursday afternoons of years ago when he would rush over here to watch the paper being printed. "Do you ever use this equipment anymore?" he asked.

"No need since I sold the paper," Jackson said, snatching up more letters from the type boxes. "Never get print jobs that big."

Surveying the bound volumes, Jay's attention focused on a book smaller than the others; a scrapbook, labeled *October 12, 1958: The Mineral Lake Murder*. His hand, almost automatically, reached out for it. He quickly thumbed through the pages, noting that this collection of yellowing clippings appeared to contain every story that Jackson had ever published in his paper about the town's most infamous crime.

"Mind if I read some of this?" he asked.

"I wish you would," Sam said.

Jay flipped through the book and stopped at an article near the back dated Friday, October 11, 1968. The lengthy piece appeared to be an overview of the entire case to date.

ANNIVERSARY OF A MURDER

Ten years ago this Sunday, a horrifying event occurred in our community from which this town has never fully recovered.

On the morning of October 12, 1958, the mutilated body of Joseph Leroy Gaston, a homeless transient, was found floating in Mineral Lake. What was left of him was being knocked against and torn by the sharp rocks below the burned out bath house off Stony Point.

There was no identification on Gaston's body. He was identified from his fingerprints, which were on file at the Department of the Army in Washington D.C. He had been born in Tulsa, Oklahoma in 1925, and had received a Purple Heart during his service in Korea. Honorably discharged from the service in 1953, he had no known relatives. He also had no criminal record.

What was Joseph Gaston doing in Mineral Lake on October 11, 1958?

We'll probably never know for sure.

Most likely, he was just passing through town, on his way to anywhere he could earn enough for his next meal.

He never got that meal, because somebody, possibly a resident of this town, put an end to his existence for a reason that we will also probably never know.

Did Joseph Gaston know his killer?

Or, was he a random victim, the target of a so-called "thrill killing"?

It's almost unthinkable that a quiet town like Mineral Lake could be the home of a "thrill killer," but that possibly does, sadly, exist.

Jay glanced up from the article. "Hey, this is good," he said to Jackson, who was inking up the type plate he'd just finished in preparation of making a proof.

"I think so," he replied.

Jay smiled, and returned to his reading.

Joseph Gaston was murdered inside the abandoned bath house. The large quantity of blood and tissue found there made that apparent. His death was brutal.

Following his autopsy, the Grant County Coroner announced that he had died from a "major trauma" to his throat. That was his unpretentious way of saying that Gaston's throat had been ripped open. The instrument of death was, quite possibly, a simple garden tool.

Jay felt a chill run down his spine, as his eyes focused on those last four words. "What kind of tool?" he asked.

"What!?!" Jackson responded, not sure of what the younger man was talking about.

"It says, 'The instrument of death was, quite possibly, a simple garden tool.' What kind of tool was it?"

"I don't know," Jackson shrugged. "One of those hand-held hoes, I think. The kind with the claws on them."

"Oh, shit!" Jay's mind began to race, as the door to a vague memory burst open. Visions flashed through his consciousness. Of Jerry Roscoe. Of the bath house ruins atop Dead Man's Bluff. And, of somebody else; his name and features clouded, like the faceless phantom in his dreams.

"What do you got?" Jackson demanded.

"*The Scarlet Claw*," Jay said.

"What scarlet claw?"

"That's why this case sounded familiar."

"What the hell are you talking about?" Jackson asked. His voice signaled annoyance.

"That's the name of one of those Basil Rathbone-Sherlock Holmes movies," replied Jay. "*The Scarlet Claw*."

"So what?" Jackson said.

"The killer in that movie used a claw-like garden tool to rip out his victims' throats."

"What does that prove?"

"Sam," Jay said, his face draining of color, "I think that I planned this murder."

Jackson smiled with disbelief. "Are you crazy!?!"

Jay slowly shook his head. "I got an even better one for you," he continued. "I think the killer is the one who has my son."

"And, who's that?" Jackson's tone was cynical.

Tears of frustration formed in Jay's eyes. "I haven't the slightest idea," he said.

TWENTY

Ed LaGrange realized that he was in over his head. He didn't know how to deal with a murder. His job was to keep the peace in Mineral Lake and little more.

True, there might be an occasional shooting in town, like the one at the Murphy Hotel last night, or like when Tom Barkley caught that airman from the nearby Moses Lake military base in the sack with his wife and shot the guy in the ass.

But even the Murphy incident was relatively simple stuff. Easy to handle.

He reflected back to that murder sixteen years ago.

He had been on duty when that transient's body was discovered in the lake, but Sam Jackson was right there, guiding him as to proper investigation procedures. And, as soon as Oscar Heath, the regular sheriff got back into town that afternoon, the matter was, thankfully, taken out of his hands and turned over to the County cops.

Now, however, he was the Sheriff, and, as Harry Truman had proclaimed, "The buck stops here!"

"I was just drivin' along," his deputy was explaining, "patrolin' like I always do...."

"How *is* Evie, Gene?" LaGrange quipped.

The deputy's expression didn't vary. "Hell," he said, "I didn't even get there yet."

LaGrange shifted his gaze to the shallow ditch next to the dirt road and studied the dust-covered, bloodied shell that was once Ralph Chaney. A gentle breeze was also blanketing the remains with shreds of grain from the nearby wheat field. He surveyed the landscape. There were no structures in sight, only wheat to the east and, across the road thin road that disappeared over the horizon, a cornfield. "Go on," he said to his deputy.

Gene rubbed at his chin. "Like I said, I was just drivin' along when I saw 'im lying here...."

"Like this?"

"Never touched a thing," Gene said, his gaze focused on LaGrange's left shoulder. "I could see he was dead. 'Besides, Huey here came along almost at the same time I did."

"I don't know nuthin' 'bout this, Sheriff," said Huey Casper, who had been leaning against the hood of his walloped Ford station wagon, listening to the lawmen. "I was just passin' by, and I saw ol' Gene stopped here."

LaGrange was not too well acquainted with Casper. He knew that he owned a goat ranch in Blue Lake Canyon, about ten miles out of town, and that he was a widower with two small kids. The red bearded, 5'4" rancher was in his mid-forties, dressed in jeans, a sport shirt and wore a black Stetson atop his head.

"You didn't touch anything?" LaGrange asked.

"Hell, no!" Casper said, craning his neck to get a better view of the corpse. "Gene told me to stay back."

"I didn't want nobody destroyin' any evidence," Gene added.

"Good thinking," LaGrange said. "I'm impressed."

"I watch enough cop shows on the television to know what to do," the deputy replied. "I'm a professional."

LaGrange avoided comment. He studied the body again. "He's been stabbed," he said. "Two or three times."

"What do we do now?" Gene asked.

"I called the County boys on the way out here," LaGrange said. "They're better qualified to handle a crime scene than we are."

"You're the sheriff," Gene nodded."

"I'm going in and break the news to Carol Chaney," LaGrange said.

"Want me to go with you?" Gene asked.

"No, you stay 'til the County guys get here. Give 'em any help they need, then join me."

"Okay."

"You were friends with Chaney, weren't you?" LaGrange asked.

Gene shrugged. "Just played cards with 'im a couple times," he said.

LaGrange opened the door of his vehicle, then suddenly looked back at the deputy. "You seen Jay Barnett around today?"

Gene shook his head. "No."

"If you spot 'im," LaGrange continued. "pick 'im up. I want to have a talk with him."

The deputy watched LaGrange's vehicle disappear down the dusty dirt road on its way back to town. "Take off, Huey," he said to the farmer, who had moved a few steps closer to the body.

"Come on, Gene," Casper objected. "Let me wait around. I never watched a real criminal investigation before."

Gene moved toward the rancher, herding him back toward his station wagon. "No way," he said. "This is an official police crime scene. No civilians allowed."

"Bullshit!"

"You want me to run you in?"

Casper assumed a demeanor of false bravado. "For what?" he demanded.

"I'll come up with something." The deputy withdrew his baton from his belt and slapped it lightly against his open palm.

"Screw you!," Casper said, climbing into his vehicle. He took off with a bolt, his rear tires discharging a cloud of dust into Gene's face.

The deputy waited until the station wagon was out of sight, then opened the trunk of his police vehicle and gathered up the blood-soaked newspapers inside.

TWENTY-ONE

Sam Jackson chewed on his cold stogie while he stared at Jay. "That's the most fantastic thing I've ever heard," he said. "Where'd you come up with a story like that?"

"It's true," Jay insisted. He paced about the back room of the print shop. "I know it sounds bizarre, but it happened like I said."

"You're telling me that you, Jerry Roscoe and this other kid, who we'll call 'Kid X,' got together one night back in the summer of 1958 and planned to kill Joe Gaston?"

"Come on, Sam!" Jay snapped. "That's out of context and you know it!"

Jackson barked back at him. "Then go slower this time," he said, "and put it into context for me."

Jay collapsed onto the stool opposite Jackson and let out a long, soft sigh. He hesitated a few moments, gathering his thoughts, then faced the former newsman.

"We were kids," he said. "Kids play games. When they're bored, like most young teens get in a dull town like this, they fantasize. They play 'What if....'

"Most of the stuff comes from TV...the movies. 'What if I was Superman...the Lone Ranger....'

"I remember that night...very well now. We were up in the bath house ruins on Dead Man's Bluff... talking about committing the perfect crime."

"The perfect crime!?!" Jackson repeated.

"There was this movie," Jay continued, ignoring the remark, "*Violent Saturday* with Victor Mature and Lee

Marvin. It was about a bank robbery. Marvin and his two henchmen were going to stick-up this small town bank.

"So, using that movie as a guide, Jerry, me and this other kid mapped out a plan to hold up the Mineral Lake Bank....Obviously, we never did it."

"If you had, I'd've put it in the paper." Jackson chuckled. "When I was that age, I planned to hold up the Southern Pacific."

"A regular Jesse James," Jay smiled. For a few seconds, he was silent. "Then," he said, finally, "we planned the perfect murder."

"Based on this Sherlock Holmes movie?"

"*The Scarlet Claw*," Jay nodded. "I think it took place in this small village in Canada. Holmes and Dr. Watson are there for some reason or another when they hear about this mysterious phantom that goes around tearing out people's throats...."

"Wonderful television you kids watched," Jackson interjected. "Your folks wouldn't let you watch 'Howdy Doody'?"

Jay ignored the sarcasm. "I think it turned out that the mailman did it. Revenge, or something. And, he was doing it with this claw-like garden tool."

"Okay," Jackson said, striking a match and attempting to re-ignite his stogie, "sounds like a great movie. What's your point?"

Jay resumed his pacing. "Let's say, that, a couple of months later, after I've gone home to Seattle, Jerry and this kid get bored and, just for the thrill of it, decide to recreate this murder. They pick up a vagrant, Joe Gaston, who's just passing through town and who nobody knows, lure him up to Dead Man's Bluff, and kill him.

"It's the perfect crime. There's no apparent motive. Nothing to connect them to the victim...."

"They just did it for the thrill?" Jackson said.

"Leopold and Loeb did it in the 1920s back in Chicago. They killed that little boy just to prove that they could get away with it. There was probably some perverse sexual motive, but...."

"Leopold and Loeb were a couple of 'queers,'" Jackson interrupted. "Jerry Roscoe wasn't 'queer.' Hell. I don't think there're any fucking 'queers' here in Mineral Lake."

"How do you know?" Jay retorted. "There's a major he-man movie star back in Hollywood that everybody in town knows is homosexual, but he keeps his sex life at a low profile and nobody says anything about it."

"Who?" Jackson asked.

"Besides," Jay continued, ignoring the question, "you don't have to be homosexual, latent or otherwise, to commit a sex crime."

"Okay," Jackson tentatively conceded, "they commit a thrill killing. Then what?"

"Let's say that, as the years pass, Jerry, who is basically a decent human being, is consumed with guilt over what he's done. He turns to alcohol, drugs.

"Let's say that, Kid X gets a bit worried. What if Jerry spills the beans? Then, they'd *both* wind up on the gallows.

"So, let's say, he arranges for Jerry to have an 'accident.' He gets him high, which wouldn't be hard to do, knocks him out and sends him and his car off a cliff. Now, Kid X is home free"

"That's a lot of 'let's says'," Jackson said.

"I got a few more for you," Jay replied. "Let's say that, one day, Kid X is driving along in his blue Chevy van, minding his own business, when he sees me in town. He panics. Why, after all these years, am I here? Is it about the murder?"

"Are you making this up as you go along?" Jackson asked, facetiously.

"Yeah," Jay said, "but it fits."

"Continue," Jackson shrugged.

"He pretends he's a newspaper reporter and calls me over at the Franklin Court to see why I'm here. I tell him I'm in town to settle a real estate deal, but he's not satisfied. What if I should learn about the murder? What if I remember that night up on Dead Man's Bluff, and put two-and-two together?"

"Why," Jackson interrupted, "would he kidnap your kid?"

"I think he wanted to get me out of town, so that I wouldn't learn about the murder."

"That doesn't make sense. If what you say is true, why wouldn't he just kill you and be done with it?"

"That's what he was going to do," Jay said, "but in Seattle...or before I got there. That way, it's a murder case for either the State cops or the Seattle police. They'd never even look toward Mineral Lake for a suspect."

Jackson smiled and shook his head. "It'd make a great movie," he said. "Think you could get Paul Newman to star in it?"

"Seriously," Jay said, "what do you think?"

"I don't know," Jackson replied. "I'd hate to believe that *my* "crime of the century" was the product of some goddamn Sherlock Holmes movie." He sucked some more on his stogie, then shrugged his shoulders. "It's a wild theory, but it does touch most of the bases...."

"So?"

"So, who is 'Kid X'?" Jackson asked. "What's his name?"

"I don't know."

"That helps." Jackson's tone was facetious. "This guy sounds like a real sickie, and you can't remember him."

"I'd just met him that day," Jay said, shutting his eyes to conjure up a mental image. "He'd only just moved into town and Jerry had just met him, too. He introduced us."

"You must recall *something*," Jackson probed.

"I think he asked a lot of questions about the Sherlock Holmes movie," Jay said. "He seemed fascinated by the story. How the killer was trapped and all that."

"What else? What did he look like?"

"I don't know," Jay said, frustrated. "His face is a blank."

"Improvise," Jackson said, his patience starting to erode.

Jay's forehead dissolved into a mass of wrinkles, as he fought to regain a distant memory. "He was a normal-looking kid, I guess. He...."

"He *what*?"

"His eyes," Jay said. "They were very cold, unfriendly. The only time they showed any life was when I was talking about the movie."

"Would you recognize him if you saw him again?"

Jay shook his head. "He could be standing right here in front of me and I wouldn't know him from Adam."

TWENTY-TWO

It all was falling apart. Chance events were occurring so quickly that the carefully devised game plan he had followed these past sixteen years was no longer working.

Gene Thomas watched the two men from the County Coroner's office load the black body bag containing Ralph Chaney's remains into the rear of their death wagon, then drive off down the dusty road toward the highway. He turned to the pair of detectives, who were still sifting the soil around the area where the body had lain, looking, he assumed, for hair, fibers and any other physical evidence.

They would find nothing. Gene had made sure of that.

"You guys still need me?" he asked, glancing at his watch. It was a quarter-to-six. The light was starting to fade.

Ryan, the older of the two men, shook his head. "You can take off," he said. "Thanks for your help."

"Tell your boss we'll call 'im tomorrow," the other man said, not looking up from his efforts.

Gene sneered at the detectives, then headed his car back toward town. He hated the fact that he was going to have to improvise, but he had something to do, and not much time in which to do it.

"*Damn Jay Barnett!*" he cursed aloud.

Why did he have to come back to Mineral Lake after all this time?

Things had been going so well. He'd been Ed LaGrange's deputy for nearly five years now. Ed liked him, and since LaGrange was planning to retire sooner or later, Gene was the likely choice to take over his job.

Evie Randall liked him, too. So did her folks. She was a little on the heavy side and her teeth were a bit crooked, but some day Randall's hundred-acre farm would belong to Edie, and she'd need a husband to help her run it.

He was going to marry her. He was also going to be sheriff. His father, the Major would've liked that. He might even have been proud.

More importantly, what had happened sixteen years ago had almost been forgotten. Folks in Mineral Lake seldom talked about the murder any more. Except for Sam Jackson. But, he'd usually had a few too many drinks when the subject came up, and nobody paid him much attention.

Gene felt no remorse for what he and Jerry Roscoe had done that night.

They'd been bored.

They did it because....

It was a lark! They wanted to give the town something to talk about, and Gene wanted to experience what his father had experienced. He wanted to know what it would feel like to kill someone.

"*Murder somebody!?!*" Jerry had been aghast when Gene had first proposed the idea.

"Not just murder," Gene had argued. "We're gonna commit 'the crime of the century,' or whatever they call it. An unsolved mystery that they'll write about in books and magazines."

"How do we do that?" Jerry had asked, his interest tentatively sparked.

"Remember that Sherlock Holmes movie your Jew friend told us about last summer? The one where the guy ripped out people's throats?"

"Yeah?"

"Wild, huh?" Gene had said. "And, we don't have to worry about no Sherlock Holmes solvin' anything."

"But, killing somebody…," Jerry said, hesitantly. "that…would be a terrible thing..."

"Who's that talkin'?" Gene had taunted. "Your mama or your bitchy old grandma?"

Jerry flushed. "They got nothin' to do with this," he said.

"Sure, they do," Gene retorted, well aware that he was prodding him where he was most vulnerable. Jerry was always complaining that he couldn't come out because his Grandma wanted him to do this, or his Mom wanted him to help out with that. "You got two women tellin' you what to do," Gene continued, "and you do it. You're not a man. You're a girl… A little Mama's girl."

"Shut up!"

"A man goes out and does what *he* wants to do," Gene persisted. "He doesn't stay home and help his grandma…do what? Wash the dishes? Clean the toilet? Sew a new dress? You'd look pretty in a dress."

Jerry's anger had him on the verge of tears, but he still wasn't convinced. "No," he said. "I won't do it."

Gene's next move was quite calculated. He spit onto the ground. "Fine," he said. "If you're that big of a chicken shit… If you don't have the guts to do something that *a man* would do… You can go to hell. I don't want to see you any more." Then, he turned around and stomped off.

"Gene?" Jerry had called to him impotently, but Gene had ignored him.

Two days later, Jerry, eyes downcast to hide the fact that he'd been weeping, had come up to Gene after school and agreed to go along with the plan.

Gene hadn't been surprised. Jerry was a lonely kid who kept to himself. Gene was his only friend… except for

Jay Barnett and Carol Franklin, but they wouldn't be back in Mineral Lake until next summer.

If the man they'd killed had been a "somebody," like a resident of the community or a person with a family, then, maybe, Gene would have felt some remorse. But, what-was-his-name? Joe Gaston! He was *a bum*. An absolute nobody. The kind of person that the Major would describe as a "dumb, useless soldier you'd send out on point when you knew that snipers were around."

They'd found Gaston out on the highway on a cold and windy night, trying to thumb a ride. All it took to lure him was the promise of a hamburger and a place to sleep for the night.

He was filthy. Probably hadn't bathed in over a week. They made him ride in the back of the pick-up they'd borrowed from Jerry's mom, telling her that they were helping a friend move a sofa.

"I don't think I can do this," Jerry had said, driving back toward town.

Gene was prepared for Jerry's retreat. "Don't worry about it," he'd assured him. "I've changed my mind, too… We'll just have some fun with the guy, then let him go."

That seemed to relieve Jerry's anxieties.

The deed had been done quickly. Up at the bath house on Dead Man's Bluff, Jerry had pretended to build a fire to cook the food. With Gaston's back turned toward him, Gene had picked up a large jagged rock and effortlessly brought it down onto the vagrant's head.

"Jesus!" Jerry had winced, turned pale, at the crunching sound. "You said that you…"

Gene's expression was like ice. "Changed my mind, again" he said. He was thankful that Jerry had not vomited. The mess might've been too difficult to clean up.

Jerry's eyes were fixed on the unconscious man. He started to move toward the exit.

"Where do you think you're going?" Gene demanded.

"I didn't do anything…," Jerry said, shaking his head. There were tears in his eyes.

"Nobody will believe you."

"But…"

"Nobody will believe you," Gene repeated.

They stared at each other for a long moment.

"What do we do, now?" Jerry had asked, finally surrendering.

"Now," Gene said, withdrawing the claw-like gardening tool from the pocket of his windbreaker, "we really have fun. Take off your clothes."

"What!?" Jerry seemed taken aback at the command.

"You want to get blood all over 'em?"

Jerry nodded, then had silently complied. They stripped without speaking. The only sounds were the wind outside and the waves lapping against the rocks below.

SQUISH!

Gene had never forgotten the sound as the garden tool tore into the unconscious man's throat.

His thoughts drifted. He thought again of his father.

The Major was quite the military man. Despite his insensitivity and cruelty, Gene was proud of his memory. In battle, he'd killed "Krauts"... "Gooks".... He had a reputation for not taking prisoners. "If the bastards want to take on the United States," he's say, "fuck 'em! Let 'em suffer the consequences."

He'd come up through the ranks. He'd won the Silver Star in France during World War II and, in Germany he snagged his first Purple Heart. Korea is where he traded his left leg and both testicles for another Purple Heart when he stepped onto a land mine. He spent the rest of his life in a wheelchair.

The family moved to Mineral Lake in 1958 when a doctor at the Los Angeles Veteran's Hospital suggested that the arthritic condition that was developing in the Major's hands might be helped by the lake's medical properties. There, the family lived off the Major's disability pay and a modest trust fund that his father, a corporate vice-president, had established for him.

Gene had never met his grandparents. Both were killed in a plane crash when the Major was still in his teens.

The Major had become a bitter man. He drank a bottle of bourbon a day, methodically recounted his military experiences, screamed at his dutiful wife and berated his son, who only wanted to emulate him.

Despite his physical condition, he was still "the Major," and he wasn't about to let anybody forget that.

"Why couldn't he ever please that old miserable son-of-a-bitch?" Gene wondered, as he reached the main highway and took a right turn toward town.

Jerry had become another "dumb, useless soldier".

They hadn't seen much of each other after that night. Jerry had avoided him. Whenever they'd crossed paths on the street or in school, Jerry looked or walked the other way.

"What the fuck are you doing?" Gene had demanded one afternoon when he'd cornered Jerry alone in the locker room after gym class. "Why are you duckin' me?"

"I... I just don't feel good 'bout what we did," Jerry'd stammered in a low voice. "We did a terrible sin."

"When did you start goin' to Sunday School?" Gene responded. "We made the front page of the Seattle papers, didn't we? The Spokane and Portland ones, too."

Jerry glanced down the row of lockers to make sure they were alone. "What if we get caught?" he said.

"The cops don't know a damn thing. The only way we can get caught is if you open your big mouth."

"I'm not sayin' nuthin'," Jerry assured him. "I just don't want to be around you for a while. That's all."

"Whatever happens to me happens to you, too," Gene warned. "They hang people in this state."

Jerry continued to avoid him. He avoided everybody. He became the school recluse. He stopped participating in school athletic activities. He didn't go to parties. He'd go directly home after classes ended, and wouldn't be seen again until the next morning when the first bell rang. He didn't even attend his own graduation ceremonies.

The first time Jerry had been arrested was for being drunk and disorderly in a public place. Almost a year after he'd finished high school, Ed LaGrange had discovered Jerry walking along the beach, shouting "Fuck," "Shit," Cocksucker" and every other cuss word he could come up with. When Ed had approached him, Jerry turned his back, unzipped his fly and urinated into the surf.

LaGrange had felt sorry for the kid, or maybe he'd just remembered the first time that he'd laid one on. He'd let Jerry sleep it off in jail that night, then drove him home the next morning and told him not to do it again.

Jerry didn't. Not for a month, at least.

Gene hadn't been around when this had all taken place. Like other kids in his high school class, he'd enlisted in the Army after graduation, and had spent six years stationed in Germany. He'd became an M.P., made sergeant and lived off base with a German girl named Elsa.

Upon his discharge, he'd bid good-bye to Elsa and returned to Mineral Lake. His parents had passed away while he'd been gone. He'd inherited their house on Maple and a sizable savings account that, along with his discharge pay, gave him plenty of time to laze around and take life easy.

Gene had run into Claude Bates the first time he'd visited the Texaco station. Claude had dropped out of high school during the middle of their junior year and joined the Navy. "Sure, Jerry Roscoe's still around," the grease-monkey had responded to Gene's question. "If he's not in the drunk tank, he's in Donlevy's Tavern, gettin' ready to go there."

Gene had stopped by Donlevy's that night. The place was nearly empty. A guy in a pair of plumber's coveralls was drinking a draft beer while he played himself a game of pool in a dreary corner of the room. A couple in their fifties sat at the bar, chatting with Bill Donlevy, the sixty-five-year-old owner/bartender. His beer belly and bulbous red nose testified to the truth of the rumor Gene had always heard about the man, that he drank up all his profits.

Emaciated, bleary-eyed and sprouting a shaggy beard, Jerry Roscoe sat alone in a back booth, staring at an empty glass that had once held a beer. A half smirk crossed his lips, as he saw Gene approach. "Hey, dude," he'd said with a wave. "When did you get back?"

Gene slid into the seat across from him and motioned Donlevy to draw two more drafts. "Few days," he answered with a smile.

"How was 'Nam?"

"Wouldn't know," Gene said. "I been stationed in Germany."

Donlevy brought over the beers. Gene paid him, then turned back to Jerry. "What've you been doin'?" he asked.

"I'm the town drunk," Jerry said with a shrug. "Haven't you heard?"

"Why's that?"

"Guess I don't like me very much."

Gene studied his former high school chum for almost a minute. "Jer," he said finally, "you ever step on a bug?"

"What?"

"Did you ever kill a bug? An insect?"

'Sure," Jerry replied, looking somewhat bewildered.
"Plenty of 'em. We used to get a kick outta pourin' kerosene
down those red ant hills then settin' 'em on fire."

"Did them bugs do any good in the world?" Gene
continued. "Did anybody miss 'em when they were gone?"

Jerry grinned. "Other bugs?" he offered.

"Aside from that?" Gene chuckled.

"Guess not."

"Same thing with that guy we did," Gene said in a
low voice. "He wasn't doin' the world no good. And, nobody
missed him."

"Yeah," Jerry had said, "but he weren't no bug. He
was a person."

That was the moment when Gene knew that he would
have to kill Jerry Roscoe.

A pale green Ford sedan turned out of the alley in
front of him.

Gene recognized the car. He knew the driver. And,
when he saw who was sitting in the passenger's seat, he knew
that his luck was still with him.

He ensconced himself in the "'Aw, shucks,' Jimmy
Stewart-like" guise that he'd adopted for the benefit of the
local citizenry, then reached up and turned on his police siren.

TWENTY-THREE

Sam Jackson had just switched on his headlights when he heard the police siren wail behind him. He looked into his rearview mirror, and saw the red light flashing atop the official vehicle. Deputy Gene Thomas was behind the wheel.

"What the hell does he want?" Jackson said, half to himself and half to Jay, who he was driving back to the Franklin Court. He stopped his car in front of the Presbyterian church.

The building was closed; dark, except for a night light. Nobody was around.

"We don't have time for this," Jay said. He was anxious to get back to the Court and talk to Carol and, if he was there, Ralph. He and Sam had agreed that the Chaneys could be in the best position to tell them who Jerry Roscoe had been "friendly with" during the final chapter of his life and, thus, who might have been responsible for his death.

"Let me take care of this," Sam said. He shut off his motor and stepped out of the vehicle. "Wait here."

Jackson saw Thomas get out of his car and unsnap the leather guard on his side holster. "What're you going to do, Gene?" he smiled. "Shoot me?"

"Just stay where you are, Mr. Jackson," the deputy said. "I don't want nobody to get hurt here."

"What!?!" Jackson responded, not quite sure he believed what he was hearing.

"That's the Barnett fella you got in the car, ain't it?"

"Yeah. Something wrong with that?"

"Sheriff wants to talk to 'im."

"That's okay," Jackson said. The deputy's caution amused him. "I'm sure he'll come peaceable."

Thomas remained poker-faced. "Maybe," he said.
He whipped his police service revolver out of his holster, and
aimed through the rear window of Jackson's car at the back of
Jay's head. "Tell 'im to step out...with his hands up."

"Gene," Jackson said, turning angry, "are you
crazy!?! What the hell is going on here?"

"What is this?" Jay asked, emerging from the car.

"Hands up!" the deputy ordered.

"Why?" A puzzled expression on his face, Jay
proffered his empty hands toward Thomas.

"'Cause I said so!"

Jay shrugged and fully extended his arms above his
head. Thomas moved over to him, his weapon ready.

"Ed LaGrange is going to have your ass, son,"
Jackson said.

"Maybe," Thomas drawled. "But, I'm just followin'
his orders." He retrieved his handcuffs from his belt. "Turn
around," he said to Jay. "Give me your hands."

Jay reluctantly obeyed. "What's the charge?" he
asked.

Thomas waited until he'd snapped on the cuffs, then
answered. "Murder."

"Who!?!" Jay and Jackson reacted in unison.

"Ralph Chaney."

Jay blanched. "He's dead!?! he gasped, turning to
face the deputy.

"Yeah, he's dead."

"When did this happen?" Jackson asked, aghast.

"Dunno for sure," Thomas said, taking Jay by the arm
and leading him back to his official vehicle. "We found 'im
out on Darby Road. He'd been stabbed to death. Coroner's
gonna let us know when."

"Why me?" Jay asked.

"Everybody knows you been boffin' Chaney's wife," the deputy said with a sneer. "Nobody here in town would've killed 'im."

"That's fuckin' bullshit," Jay snapped. "We're just friends."

"Sure," Thomas snickered.

"I gotta talk to Carol," Jay said. "I got a right to do that, don't I?"

"Maybe, later." He sat his prisoner down into the back seat of his car and shut the door.

"Where are you taking him?" Jackson asked.

"To see the sheriff," Thomas said. "You can follow us if you want." He slid behind the wheel.

"I will," Jackson said. "Because this is pure crap."

"Won't you just take me over to see Carol?" Jay asked, half pleading, as the deputy started his engine. "I'm not going to try to escape."

"Sorry," Thomas said. "Can't do that." He headed the car west.

Jay realized that appealing to this dunce was a waste of breath. He let out a sigh, plopped back onto the seat and looked through the rear window. Sam was following about a half block behind them.

"You don't really think I killed Ralph Chaney, do you?" he asked the deputy.

"Dunno." Thomas kept his eyes on the road.

"Christ, I haven't seen Carol in sixteen years. I come to town and two days later I kill her husband! That sure makes a lot of sense."

"Strange things like that happen," Thomas said. "Why did you come back to town?"

"To close a business deal. I'd've been out of here the next day, but the guy I was meeting got delayed."

"Too bad for you."

"Yeah," Jay sneered, "Too bad." He studied the back of the deputy's head for a few moments before he spoke again. "You lived here long," he asked.

"Since I was in my teens." Thomas hung a right, heading the vehicle down toward the lake.

"You know Jerry Roscoe?"

"Uh-huh."

"Who'd he hang out with? Do you know?"

"Jerry was pretty much of a loner." The deputy made another right turn, then took a quick left up a winding rock encrusted road that, as Jay recalled, was the back way up to the old bathhouse atop Dead Man's Bluff.

"Why are we going up here?" Jay asked with some apprehension. He glanced out the back window. Sam was still right behind them.

"This is where we found the body," Thomas said. "Sheriff's still investigatin'."

"They found him *here*!?!" Jay's mind began racing once again, as he struggled to comprehend the uncanny coincidence. "Do all your murders happen here?" he asked sarcastically.

"Not all," the deputy said. He stopped the car at the top of the incline. Up ahead about thirty yards, Jay could make out the bath house ruins illuminated by the moonlight. No other vehicles were in sight, except for....

Jay squinted his eyes. Was that a Chevy van parked in the shadows of the ghastly rock structure?

Thomas opened the car door, as he reached down under his seat and grabbed what appeared to be a small folded brown paper bag. "Just the ones that you plan," he said with a smirk. He slammed the door and walked back toward Sam's Ford, idling behind them. Jackson got out of his sedan.

"The ones that *I* plan...." Jay pondered to himself. "How did he know...?"

He looked again at the ruins. That was the blue
Chevy van parked there. And then, he knew.

His thoughts were interrupted by Sam's angry voice
behind him. "What're you draggin' us up here for?" Jackson
bellowed.

Jay was maneuvering around in the seat, turning his
head to look out the back window, when he heard a sound
with which he'd become very familiar during the past two
days.

POP!

He saw Sam Jackson's form slam up against the hood
of his car, then slip down onto the ground out of his sight.
From the spill of the headlights, he could make out what
appeared to be splotches of red covering the Ford's
windshield.

A few feet away, Gene Thomas stood holding that
brown paper bag, which now had a black smoking hole in it.

The deputy looked over in Jay's direction and
appeared to smile.

TWENTY-FOUR

"He has a *son*!?!" Ed LaGrange said, his tone still incredulous.

For the past half hour, he'd been sitting in the Chaney kitchen, listening to a distraught Carol Chaney relate the unusual events of Jay Barnett's visit to Mineral Lake. He didn't really give much credence to her fantastic tale of a mysterious kidnapping, but she appeared to believe it. The girl, he thought, was just too broken up over her husband's death to be thinking clearly.

"Have you ever seen this kid?" he continued.

Carol dried her eyes with a tissue. "Of course I have," she said. He's a nice little boy."

She started to reach for the telephone. "I've got to call Randy," she said with a fresh sob. "He needs to know about his father."

LaGrange stepped between her and the phone. "In a minute," he said. His tone was gentle, but remained firm. "Answer me some questions first."

"What?"

"Did Jay tell you about his financial problems?"

"I know he needs money," Carol said, "but that's why he came here. To pick up a check from the bank."

"You don't think his kid's disappearance is part of an insurance scam. To raise some quick cash?"

"Where'd you ever get that idea?" she blurted.

LaGrange shrugged. "I just know he's up to something."

"He's up to getting his son back!" Carol shouted.

"The boy's name? What is it?"

"David."

"And, he's been kidnapped?"

"That's right."

"You know that for certain?"

"Sure, I do," Carol said, testily. "How could you think that Jay would make up something like that?"

"I don't know what he'd do," LaGrange said.

"If he wasn't afraid to go to you," Carol said, "then maybe Ralph wouldn't've gotten involved, and maybe he'd still be alive." She suddenly stopped to ponder her words.

"You've thought of something?" LaGrange asked.

"That's it!" Carol said. "Ralph must've known something, and he went off to explore it on his own."

"Like what?"

"Like who in town rides around in a blue Chevy van?"

LaGrange started to reply, then hesitated. "Why a blue Chevy van?" he asked.

"Because Jay thinks that's what the kidnapper is driving."

"Jesus!" LaGrange muttered.

"You know somebody who has one?"

"My deputy," the sheriff shrugged," but he...."

"Gene Thomas!" Carol interrupted. "Ralph used to play poker over at his house. He only lives two or three blocks from us."

LaGrange shook his head. "Gene's an honest, hardworking guy," he said. "Comes from a good family. He wants my job when I retire....

"Frankly," he mused, "I don't think he's smart enough to plan a kidnapping."

"Jay said that the kidnapper told him that he would know if the police were called in." Carol insisted. "That fits. Gene would know."

"Yeah, but...."

"Where's Gene, now?"

"I told him to finish up at the crime scene where we found Ralph, then to...." The sheriff contemplated for a moment. "Hell," he continued, "he might be out looking for Jay. I told him to bring him in if he could."

"Oh, my God!" Carol said. "Do you know what that means? If Gene is the kidnapper and he finds Jay, he's going to kill him."

LaGrange emitted an anxious chuckle. "Why would he do that?"

"Because," Carol said, "he's gotta know now that Jay's been talking, and the only way he can be sure that he doesn't talk any more, or figure out for himself what this thing...this kidnapping...is all about...is to kill him."

The sheriff looked at her without speaking. He didn't know what to think. "Let's take a run over to Gene's," he said finally.

TWENTY-FIVE

"Your son is fine, Thomas assured his prisoner, still handcuffed in the rear seat of the sheriff's car. "He's in the back of my van, safe and sound."

Jay continued to struggle, kicking at the door. "Let me see him, you son-of-a-bitch!"

"In a minute," the deputy said, his Jimmy Stewart guise having vanished. "First, we talk."

"I want to see my son!" Jay demanded.

Thomas' voice was calm. "Shut the fuck up," he said, shining his flashlight into Jay's eyes, "or I'll kick the little brat's teeth out."

"I'LL KILL YOU!" Jay screamed.

"No, you won't," Thomas said. "You'll listen. You'll do what I say. I'm in control."

Jay remained silent for a long moment, weighing his limited options. He took a deep breath before he finally spoke in almost a whisper. "Why did you kill Sam?"

"Wrong place. Wrong time," Thomas said. "I can't have witnesses, can I?"

"You're going to kill me?"

Thomas shrugged an affirmative.

"And my son?"

"We'll see."

"He doesn't know anything," Jay said. "He can't hurt you."

"He's a smart little kid," Thomas said. "Now, I got some questions."

"Go fuck yourself!"

"Don't fuck with me!" Thomas spat back. "Your kid is mine. You'll give me the answers."

Jay's reply was sullen. "Ask."

"Who else knows?"

"Knows what?"

"About the infamous Mineral Lake murder?"

"Nobody," Jay said. "I figured the whole thing out just now while I was at Sam's shop."

"What exactly did you figure out."

"That you, me and Jerry Roscoe planned it way back when. Then, sometime later, you and Jerry carried it out."

"You're a very clever guy, Barnett." Thomas said. "I was afraid when I saw you going into the bank the other day that something like this would happen."

"You're the one that called me at the Franklin Court," Jay said. "Pretended that you were a reporter."

"I had to know why you were here."

"I was here to close a business deal. I'd never even heard about the murder until that night."

"Probably," Thomas agreed. "But, then you saw me when I responded to the call about yer car.

"You know, I was so worried 'bout that that I almost torched yer cabin."

"Then it wasn't a dream," Jay said. "I did smell gasoline."

"Lucky for you, you woke up, or you would've been charred meat long ago."

"I didn't know who the fuck you were," Jay said. "Just some dumb hick cop."

"Not that dumb," Thomas said. "I did the perfect murder sixteen years ago. I did it again with Jerry when I got him drugged up and sent him and his car flyin' off that cliff. And, I'm gonna do it one more time with Ralph Chaney and Sam there."

"How's that?"

Thomas chuckled. "*You* did it," he said, holding up the brown paper bag with the black hole in it. He tore away the paper and grasped the .45. "You did it with Ralph Chaney's own gun."

"Bullshit!"

"Bet ballistics will show it's the same one he shot poor Sean Murphy with...while he was aimin' at you."

"Where'd you get it?"

"I took it off ol' Ralph," Thomas continued, "after I found him snoopin' around inside my house. He'd found yer little brat, so I really had no choice."

The deputy guffawed again. "Too bad," he said. "I could always beat him big in poker."

"You're crazy!" Jay knew he had to stall this whacko until he could figure a way out of this danger. "Why would I kill Ralph?" he asked.

"'Cause he found out you were boffin' his wife and you had to get rid of him. Hell, after he shot at you, maybe you figured you had no choice."

Jay forced himself to smile. "You'll never convince anybody of that," he said, wondering how he was going to get this asshole to remove the handcuffs.

"You won't be around to say otherwise," Thomas said. "And, my boss can be pretty gullible sometimes."

"This was never a kidnapping for ransom," Jay said. "You just wanted me out of town."

"You got it right," the deputy replied.

"And, you were going to ambush me on the road?"

"Jesus, but you're smart," Thomas said. "But, then you started telling me 'bout yer not havin' any money before Monday, and I was stuck with my story. Had to improvise. I hate to improvise, but I am pretty good at it."

"Can I see my son, now?"

"Sure can," Thomas said. He opened the car door. "You sure you didn't tell Carol Chaney nuthin'?"

Jay scooted along the seat and put his feet onto the ground. "I told you '*no*,'" he said, ducking his head as he stood up.

"I hope not. Hate to have to improvise with her, too." He took Jay's arm and started to escort him up the mild gravel slope toward the van.

"Okay," Jay said, "let's just say that you do convince Ed LaGrange that I did kill Ralph. Why would I kill Sam, too?"

Once again, Thomas chuckled. "That's easy," he said. "He found out about Ralph, and you had to 'do' him. Makes sense, don't it?"

"Then, you come along and 'do' me?"

"You got it. Too bad I wasn't in time to save poor Sam."

Jay turned to face Thomas. "How are you going to explain my son?" he asked.

"That was a real tragedy," Thomas said with mock emotion. "You saw me. Panicked. Tried to escape in Sam's car. Ran the damn thing off Dead Man's Bluff. Poor little kid was in the back seat."

"Very clever, Jay said, "except how can I do that with my hands cuffed behind my back?"

"They'll come off...afterwards."

"Won't work," Jay beamed. "You gotta take 'em off before you 'do' me. Otherwise, there's going to be marks on my wrists."

Thomas beamed back at him. "Not if the car catches fire and the body's burned up."

"You think you're going to be able to get them off me after that?" Jay asked, hoping that the deputy wouldn't detect his fear. He pushed himself to maintain his self-satisfied grin. "The heat will cause the metal to adhere to my skin."

"Yeah?" Thomas pondered. "How do you know that?"

"I read, shmuck." Jay could sense a sudden uncertainty within his captor. "When they do an autopsy on me, they'll find that," he pressed.

"Then, we'll have to improvise something else," Thomas said.

Jay could almost hear the wheels turning inside of the deputy's head. "You've painted yourself into a corner, fella," he said. "You're piling on layer upon layer of bullshit, and there's no way you're going to convince anybody of this convoluted story you're...*improvising*."

"You're right!" Thomas said. "So, maybe we'll just have you and your kid and Sam just disappear."

"Disappear!?!" Jay felt a chill pass through his body. "Where?" he asked.

"How should I know," Thomas smiled. "I didn't see where you went." He pulled some keys from his pocket, unlocked the rear door of the blue Chevy van, then took a flashlight from his belt and switched it on. "Don't get too excited, now," he said, opening the door. He directed the beam inside the vehicle.

Jay peered into van. "You fucking son-of-a bitch!" he exploded, kicking out at Thomas. The deputy jumped back to avoid the blow.

Jay started to lose his balance, and braced himself against the van to avoid falling. His footing recovered, he gazed again inside of the Chevy.

David lay on his belly on the floor of the van, partially covered by a mud-caked tarp. He was gagged and hog-tied. Petrified with fear, the child's eyes brightened when he saw his father.

"Untie him!" Jay demanded.

The deputy shrugged. "Can't do that," he said.

"You can take the gag out of his mouth, can't you?"

"I could."

"Then do it," Jay said. "Please!"

Thomas appeared to be amused. "Promise to be good? Not to try anything funny?"

"Yeah," Jay said, sullenly. "I give you my word." Stupid as it might seem, he knew what he was going to do. He took two steps backward, giving his captor some distance between them, then lowered his head slightly.

"That's good enough for me," Thomas said. He thrust Chaney's .45 into his belt, then, pushing aside a shovel and pick-ax that lay on the van floor, he placed his right foot onto the bumper.

As the deputy stepped up into the van, Jay, like a fighting bull attacking a matador in the ring, suddenly charged. He caught the man in mid-air. His head plowed into Thomas' mid-section, knocking the wind out of him and sending him sprawling onto his back.

"I lied!" Jay shouted, maintaining his balance. He gave the deputy a hard swift kick in the crotch. "How's that feel, you cock-sucking bastard?" Thomas screamed with pain and grabbed at his injured genitals.

Another kick caught him under the chin, knocking his head back onto the ground. Jay moved quickly up to the deputy's head, raised his foot and brought his heel down hard onto his face. Again, Thomas shrieked as the bridge of his nose crumbled.

Jay delivered one last swift kick to the deputy's temple. The man lay silent.

"Jesus," Jay said to himself, as he stared down at the still form of his tormentor, "I didn't know I had that in me."

He squatted, his back to the prone figure, and, with his hands still cuffed behind him, reached down inside Thomas' pocket. His perspiring, cramped fingers found what they were seeking. The deputy's keys. After a couple of false starts, Jay managed to get a firm grip on them. He maneuvered himself to his feet and hurried to the van.

He could see that the child had been weeping, but his eyes brightened when he saw his father.

"It's going to be okay, Daver," Jay assured his son. He braced himself against the side of the van door, then slid on his butt inside the vehicle. "I'm going to untie you, then you're going to unlock my hands, then the two of us are going to get the hell out of here and call the police." His back to the boy, Jay reached over and pulled the gag down from his mouth.

David coughed, then coughed again. "That man is the police, Dad," he said fearfully.

Still working blind, Jay explored the cord that bound his son's hands. "No, he isn't," he said. "He just thinks he is."

Gene Thomas awoke, gagging on his own blood. He couldn't breathe through his nose. His entire head felt like it had been run over by a bulldozer.

He sat up and coughed a mouthful of blood onto the ground. The red goo bubbled on the dirt and gravel. He stared at it, struggling to collect his thoughts.

Barnett, that son-of-a-bitch, had jumped him. He'd knocked him out, and now he was gone. Gene knew he was in deep shit, unless he could catch Barnett and his brat before they....

He thought he heard voices. They sounded like they were coming from the Chevy. The door was still open. Maybe, just maybe, his luck hadn't run out yet.

Slowly, he pushed himself up, planting his feet onto the ground, while he paused for his head to stop pounding. He unsnapped his holster, then, service revolver in hand, moved quietly toward the vehicle.

"Improvise," he mouthed to himself.

Behind him, a pair of headlight beams were becoming visible, as they headed up the winding road toward the top of the bluff.

Jay felt the handcuffs "click" open.

"Good job, Daver," he said, rubbing his wrists. He spun around, took the key from his son and unlocked the other bracelet. Freeing the boy's feet from the cord only took a few more seconds. "Let's get the hell out of here."

He took David up into his arms and moved swiftly to the van entrance. "Were those headlights coming up the bluff?" he wondered to himself. He decided to head in that direction.

Stepping down onto the ground, Jay felt a sharp blow to his right side. He lost his balance. Father and son went sprawling onto the gravel. A sharp rock cut into Jay's palm.

He looked up. Thomas, foot primed to deliver another blow, stood over him. "My turn," Thomas said.

David screamed.

"How do you like it?" the deputy snarled, his voice approaching hysteria. He relaxed his foot and positioned his service revolver an inch from Jay's forehead. "You're dead! Both of you!"

Again, Jay surprised even himself. He remained calm. "You got company," he said. He pointed to the headlights that were just topping the rise behind Thomas.

"*Shit!*" Thomas spat, squinting at the beams. He retreated two steps into the shadows at the side of the van.

Jay sensed that the deputy wasn't sure what to do next. He clutched a handful of gravel, then shifted his weight so that he could scramble quickly to his feet.

The still indistinguishable automobile pulled up next to Sam Jackson's car and stopped. The driver's door opened and an obscure figure hurried back behind the vehicle.

"*Oh, my God!*" they heard a horrified Ed LaGrange say. "*Sam!*"

Thomas cocked the hammer of his service revolver. He reached down and grabbed David by the collar of his already torn shirt.

"*Daddy!*" the boy cried. Thomas wrapped his arm around his neck.

"Let him go!" Jay demanded. He pushed himself to his feet. "It's over!"

"It's over when I say it's over," Thomas barked.

"Gene?" LaGrange called. "Are you up here?" The sheriff walked to the front of his vehicle. He was silhouetted by the headlights.

Jay smiled with relief. "It's over!" he repeated to Thomas. "You can't kill everybody."

"Shut up!"

"You'll run out of improvisations."

"Maybe, then, I'll just kill you." Thomas said, perspiration glistening on his forehead.

"What's going on?" LaGrange called.

"I got Barnett here," Thomas shouted. "He killed Chaney and Sam Jackson."

"I don't think so, Gene," La Grange said. "I've been to your house."

"You been to my house!?!"

Jay kept his hand filled with gravel pressed to his side. He took a short step toward David.

"Looked like a damn slaughterhouse," LaGrange continued. "Blood all over the place."

"*Shit!*" Thomas glowered at Jay. "You did this!"

Jay failed to conceal his surprise. "Me!?!"

"Everything was goin' just fine," Thomas said, "'til you came back."

"Well, I'm sorry." Jay said.

"Come on down, Gene," LaGrange called. He took a step toward them. "I'll do what I can for you."

"You'll do *nuthin'*!" Thomas shouted. He released his grip on David, pointed his revolver toward LaGrange and fired.

POP!

The bullet whizzed over the sheriff's head, who ducked for cover next to his car.

Jay leaped forward, grabbing David with his free hand and pulling him away from Thomas' reach. The deputy responded by turning his weapon toward him.

Jay flung the gravel into Thomas' face. The deputy shrieked. He grabbed at his eyes, dropping his weapon. Jay tackled him and the pair went sprawling onto the ground. "*Run, Daver!*" Jay shouted. "*Run!*"

The child hesitated, then, instead of dashing down the incline toward LaGrange, still crouched beside his vehicle, he scurried around the side of the bath house.

"*No!*" Jay yelled, pinning Thomas to the ground, "The other way!"

David didn't hear him.

Jay panicked. He knew that he had to get after his son. If he didn't, the boy might just keep racing into the darkness until he ran off the cliff and fell onto the rocks below.

He smashed his right fist into Thomas' bloodied face, but the deputy managed to bring up his knee, catching him in the groin.

With Jay grasping his middle, Thomas bolted to his feet, snatched his service revolver up off the ground, then darted around the bath house after the boy.

Jay agonizingly pushed himself up and staggered after his foe.

Behind the bath house, there was only night. Jay could hear Thomas' footsteps, but all he saw were fleeting shadows. "David!" he called. "Hide! Wait 'til I come for you."

POP!

The flash from Thomas' revolver exploded in the blackness. What felt like a spitball nicked Jay on the side of his right arm. He reached up and touched something warm and sticky oozing through his shirt.

POP!

Another flash. Jay heard the bullet whiz past his head. He dropped down into a crouch and listened.

Waves lapping against rocks.

Footsteps.

A soft whimper from David, then a sudden cry.

"Well, well, well...," he heard Thomas say with a deranged sounding glee.

He could see them now, dim outlines against the ebony sky. Thomas had grabbed David and was holding him up by the collar.

"Watch this, Barnett!" the deputy called pointing the barrel of his revolver at the boy's head. The hammer of the weapon clicked back.

"*No!*" Jay shouted, springing to his feet.

There was a crunch on the gravel behind him. He started to turn.

POP!

EPILOGUE

1996

Jay typed "The End," then leaned back into his padded desk chair and stared at the screen of his Mac Powerbook.

It was complete. After more than twenty years, he'd finally been able to finish his novel about what had happened in Mineral Lake.

He had dabbled with the work from time to time, but after completing a preliminary draft of the first dozen chapters, his interest had drifted to other projects. Perhaps the subject was too personal. Too painful. Whatever the reason, as far as this story was concerned, he'd experienced the world's greatest case of writer's block.

Novels, he'd rationalized, were just not his area of expertise. His writing gift was the spoken word. Dialogue. Since the debut of his "art" film, *Repercussions*, in February of 1975, he'd written and/or directed eleven major films and two Broadway plays that proved it.

He knew the real reason. To complete the novel meant looking deep within himself; revisiting his old fears; his old failings. That wasn't the happiest of tasks.

It was much easier to knock out a work of total fiction, particularly since the studios paid so generously these days for his original screenplays.

The news of Ed LaGrange's death six weeks ago had changed all that. Jay had heard that the retired lawman suffered from prostate cancer, but it was still a shock when the end actually came. Yet, it had given him the motivation to go back to his novel; to plow right through and finish it.   He owed Ed that much. The man had, after all, saved his and David's lives.

It was Ed LaGrange who had followed him around the bath house that night and shot Gene Thomas before the unstrung deputy could put a bullet into David's head. Thomas had been propelled backward; off of the bluff into the lake.

Next morning, his body, battered by the rocks, had been fished out of the water at approximately the same spot where LaGrange and Sam had found Joseph Leroy Gaston back in 1958. Poetic justice.

Later, Jay learned that LaGrange and Carol had checked out Gene Thomas' house. In the bedroom, they had found enough blood and other evidence to convince the sheriff that his trusted deputy was not all that he appeared to be.

The reality of seeing that room where Ralph had, apparently, been murdered had shaken Carol. Ed dropped her off at the Franklin Court with instructions to phone the State Police, then he had gone looking for Thomas.

His first stop, luckily, had been the bath house, because Carol had told him that the bluff and burned-out ruins had been their "secret place" as kids.

Ed had never shot anybody before that night. He'd never even drawn his gun on a suspect.

Jay looked at his watch. 7:30am. He'd have to wake the wife up in a half hour, so they could drag themselves down to LAX and pick up David.

David had been in St. Louis, performing with his rock group. He was flying in this morning to attend the wedding.

"My son, the rock star," Jay chuckled to himself.

He clicked the mouse, and the first hard copy of his book began popping out of the laser printer.

218

The aftermath of the Mineral Lake ordeal was almost as horrendous as the events themselves. Jay would've liked to have stayed awhile with Carol, seen her through her grief and also attended Sam's funeral, but he felt that it was more important to get David out of town and back home just as soon as the State Police finished grilling him, and he picked up his money at the bank.

He kept his promise to his son, however. Monday afternoon was spent at the Storyman's abode. Jay watched the old timer come alive again, as David sat at his side, totally enthralled with his true and tall tales.

Jay had no idea whether the rumors that this magical old man had molested a child were true or not, but at that moment, it made no difference.

Father and son were packed and ready to depart for Seattle on Tuesday morning when some attorney from Ephrata handed Jay a subpoena.

Maggie Murphy was suing him for damages caused to her hotel.

"This will go away," Ed LaGrange assured Jay. "I'll talk to the old bitch. Sean still has to answer for that paint job on your car."

Ed called him in Los Angeles two days later. The case had been dropped.

Helen, David's mother, didn't make life any easier for him either. "How could you have let him get kidnapped!?!" she'd demanded to know. "If you can't take care of your son, then he shouldn't be with you."

"Mom," David argued in his defense, "Dad saved me!"

"He damn well better have!"

Helen dropped the subject a week or two later. David wound up spending a couple of years seeing a shrink, and if he had any residual scars from the incident, except for an occasional nightmare, they certainly weren't apparent now.

Jay had also found himself back on the analyst's couch. "It's amazing," he told his therapist, "I've always tried to steer clear of confrontations. I avoid them like the plague...especially physical ones. Afraid that I'd get hurt. I know that comes from my relationship with my father.

"I think I'm over that, now. When the chips were down, I just reacted. There was no time for fear."

"That's what happens," the therapist explained. "It happens in battle. That's how we get war heroes. It happens when a mother sees her child pinned under a car and, suddenly, she develops superhuman strength and lifts it."

"It's okay to feel fear, Jay had continued, "but you can't let that fear stop you from doing what you have to do."

"A healthy philosophy."

Jay grinned. "My problem, now," he said, "is that I almost look for trouble. I'm going around with a chip on my shoulder with the attitude, 'Don't mess with me.'"

"That could become dangerous," the shrink said. "Be careful who you call out."

"Nobody *bigger* than me."

Six months after Jay had returned to Los Angeles. He'd gone back to Mineral Lake. Claude Bates was still pumping gas, Maggie was nowhere to be seen and Carol was still running the Franklin Trailer Court.

He started perusing the manuscript, marking grammatical errors, changing a word here and there. It read better than he thought it would. "Maybe I've got something here," he said to himself.

"You finished it?"

Jay swiveled around in his chair. His wife was standing in the doorway, dressed in her pink negligee, holding a mug of coffee. Even without makeup and her auburn hair awry, she still looked gorgeous to him. "Uh-huh," he said. "It's not bad either."

"Your stuff is *always* good," Carol said. "You just hate it when you're writing it."

Jay laughed. "It's much better to *have written*," he said, setting the pages onto his desk. "Have you talked to Randy?"

"Just now," Carol said. "He's very nervous."

"He's getting married," Jay said, going to her. "He *should* be."

"Oh," Carol replied, sporting a mock frown, "is marriage such a horrendous experience?"

"Come join me in the shower and I'll tell you."

"We took a shower together yesterday," Carol said. She allowed him to lead her toward the stairs.

"And, was it such a horrendous experience?"

"Monstrous!"

Arm-in-arm, they climbed the stairs.

THE END

In memory of The Storyman:

He kindled the imagination of

A young future storyteller.